AS WE BREAK

JACK HUNT

DIRECT RESPONSE PUBLISHING

ISBN-13: 978-1726039703
ISBN-10: 1726039706

Also By Jack Hunt

The Renegades
The Renegades 2: Aftermath
The Renegades 3: Fortress
The Renegades 4: Colony
The Renegades 5: United
Mavericks: Hunters Moon
Killing Time
State of Panic
State of Shock
State of Decay
Defiant
Phobia
Anxiety
Strain
Blackout
Darkest Hour
Final Impact
And Many More…

Dedication

For my family.

Prologue

Hours Before System Failure

A stabbing headache jolted him awake.

With it came blindness, which scared him even more.

"Hello?" he croaked. His throat was dry and breathing shallow.

A clanging sound like heavy boots against steel reverberated nearby.

Disoriented, Blake Dawson blinked and squinted trying to make sense of his surroundings. *Why can't I see?* Material tickled his nose. There was something coarse covering his head. A burlap sack? A pillowcase? He tried to move but couldn't as something sharp cut into his skin. His wrists were bound.

That's when it all came back: driving home from work, stopping at the side of a road to assist a woman who'd broken down, being grabbed from behind and a stinging sensation in his neck. They had injected him with a needle.

He'd heard voices then it all went black.

His mind instantly pieced together the rest.

The hours after returned in almost a dreamlike state — tires crunching gravel, the steady thump of helicopter rotor blades, a hard wind whipping at his clothes, the sound of waves, and the clang of steel beneath boots.

How long had he been here? One, maybe two days?

Where am I?

That was the first thing he'd asked when his captors tore off his hood and shone a blinding light in his eyes. They didn't want him to know. They refused to answer questions and the only mercy they'd shown was offering him water.

As he focused on the memory it got clearer.

Cutting his binds they pushed his chair in front of a table with multiple computer screens and instructed him on what he was to do.

"You're going to bring it down. Bring it all down," a voice said from behind a white mask with a wide smile, rosy cheeks and mustache. It came out in broken English with a hint of Russian. He instantly recognized the mask. It was Guy Fawkes, the same mask worn by Anonymous, the international hacking group.

"You're not them… are you?" Blake asked.

"Shut up and do as you're told."

Anonymous would have never brought him in to do this. They were a high-level hacktivist group across the globe that had already demonstrated their ability to perform the seemingly impossible. They didn't need to stoop to this level.

These guys were amateurs, wannabe hackers or just incapable of performing this task. Blake scanned the computer monitors in front of him trying to make sense of it.

"What do you want?" he asked.

"Your skills."

"For?"

"To take down the Internet, then the communication network, and then the entire U.S. power grid."

Blake shook his head. It wasn't that it couldn't be done, or that he couldn't do it — it was the legality of it all. At one time he would have jumped at the challenge simply for the bragging rights but that was when he was full of ego, young and stupid. He had put all that behind him. His years of illegal hacking were a thing of the past, a distant memory, nothing more than old headlines and a smear on his record. He'd done his time. Five years to be exact, back in the '90s.

He had a life now, a family, and a successful security consulting firm. There was no way in hell he was going to risk his freedom again, not for money, not for fame, not for anyone.

"Are you out of your mind?" Blake bellowed.

The sound of a gun cocking and the pressure of a cold barrel against the side of his temple answered that. He gritted his teeth and stared back at the screen before shaking his head.

"Why?"

He just wanted to know the reason. It would be several days before he would get an answer.

"Begin!"

He should have been terrified in that moment but he wasn't. Out of all the people they could have used they'd picked him. Why? Of course there was the obvious reason — he was a high-profile convicted hacker. His previous mistakes had landed him on the FBI's Most Wanted list back in the day. His crimes of wire fraud, unauthorized access of federal computers, interception of electronic communications and damage to data became the stuff of legends. But that wasn't it. His notoriety might have gained global attention and made him the fodder of hacking forums for years to come but there were others out there, thousands who had the same skills, if not better.

Blake looked back at the screen and shook his head. "No," he answered.

He was well aware that he was gambling his life and there was a high probability they would squeeze the trigger but in his fifty-two years of being alive, he'd gained a nose for sniffing out bullshit. These guys weren't the decision makers. They weren't the ones pulling the strings. Who was behind this? Who chose him and why? He wanted to speak to them.

The guy holding the gun pushed it harder against his temple.

"Do it. Now!"

"No," he replied with greater conviction.

It was the wrong response. Blake felt the brunt force of metal striking his face knocking him out of the chair. A heavy boot pressed down on his neck, then released as he was brought back up again.

"Do it."

He hesitated for a couple of seconds then refused again.

From that moment on, he was put through a cycle of punishment that he could only imagine was similar to what prisoners in Guantánamo Bay might endure: multiple beatings were followed by waterboarding, and threats of death.

Time ceased to exist.

Then it got worse.

Then it abruptly ended.

He wasn't sure how long they were out of the room, only when they returned he could hear a female crying. The bag was torn from his head once again and there before him was his wife, Kelly.

They had forced her onto her knees with her hands tied behind her back.

"No!" he cried out as they sat him in a seat and wheeled him in front of a computer.

"Do it!" they demanded.

"Blake?" she muttered as she looked up through tears.

"Kelly, it's going to be okay."

A hard crack to the side of his face and another demand, "Do it!"

Blood trickled out the corner of his mouth and for a minute he considered going through with it but it was only the knowledge that they hadn't killed him that kept him from stepping over the line. He knew the weight of the consequences. This was all just a ruse. A means to get him to give in. He figured they wouldn't harm her otherwise they would jeopardize what little hope they had of him fulfilling their demand.

He was wrong.

"No," he replied.

There was no warning given, no think again.

The guy beside her raised the gun, and squeezed the trigger.

One second she was screaming, the next silent.

It wasn't happening. It was a dream. It had to be a nightmare. He'd wake up any second now and be at home curled up beside her and she would tell him that everything was okay and to go back to sleep.

Except it never happened.

It was real.

"NO!" Blake yelled shaking from side to side in the chair, struggling to get free of his restraints. They weren't going to cut them loose until he agreed to their demand. Two of the men dragged out Kelly's body leaving behind a trail of blood on the steel floor. For a second he got a glimpse of the outside, a corridor, but that was it. Everything about what he was in

reminded him of a submarine. The metal surrounding him was industrial, military grade, the kind of setup that might have been put together back in the Second World War.

The same guy wearing the mask moved in and slapped him around the face.

"Hey, hey! Pay attention. You think that's bad?" His captor fished into his pocket and pulled out a cell phone and tapped the front a few times then twisted it around.

Blake's stomach sank.

There before him was a photo of his thirteen-year-old son.

"You want Aidan to join her?"

The question was direct and to the point. They weren't playing games. This was the real deal. They weren't going to give in any more than he was. The guy slapped Blake a few more times then shoved the chair back under the table, took out a knife and cut the zip ties holding his hands behind his back.

As soon as he was free, Blake latched onto him, clawing at him for what he'd done to Kelly but it didn't last. The man gripped a clump of Blake's hair and slammed his face into the table then held him there. His captor got real close. So close he could smell his breath. The mask touched Blake's ear as the Russian spoke again.

"Enough. This is your last chance. Do this or he dies."

Blake had no choice. Aidan was all he had left.

Any hesitation or doubts about their intentions were gone.

It was one thing to be beaten, another to see his family harmed.

"I'll do it."

Three words sealed America's fate.

He understood it would lead to a loss of life beyond any war.

Thousands would die because of his actions. That's why he'd resisted, held off as long as he could. Blake glanced over at the blood smear on the floor and a wave of guilt washed over him. His only hope was that America's greatest minds would find a way to reverse it, to turn back what he was about to do.

Blake snapped back into the present. Days had passed since he'd brought it all down, and he was still here.

What more could they want from him?

Why were they keeping him alive?

He had to escape. The question was how?

Since arriving they had kept him bound only releasing him when he needed to relieve himself, or when it came time to eat. They'd brought in a doctor twice to tend to his wounds; he assumed the doctor was there by force because she didn't wear a mask. The doc assured him that he would heal up in no time. No time? Those assholes had rearranged his face, broken his nose, knocked out two teeth, brought him to the brink of death twice and now all he could taste was blood.

The only upside was they no longer kept a hood over his face.

He was in a cramped room that looked like the quarters on a military ship, a steel box — low ceilings, one bulb behind a protective cage, steel rivets holding together the walls and floor, and a door that was locked from the other side. Even if he could get out, where would he go? He had no idea where he was. Lying on a bed he stared up at the ceiling then around his quarters. There wasn't much to it. It was windowless, stuffy and besides the bed, chair and table that was it. After he'd satisfied their demands they'd removed all the computer equipment from the room leaving it bare.

He'd thrashed around multiple times trying to break free of the restraints, even trying to cut them loose by using the steel bedpost but that only led to more pain.

Soon his thoughts turned to the doctor. She'd looked nervous on both occasions, as if she had been threatened. The look of horror on the first visit was a clear giveaway.

Maybe she could help him?

Although he hadn't seen his captors' faces he'd been able to distinguish that there were three of them by their voices. If there were more why hadn't they been in to see him the day he hacked the system? He'd seen one of them out the corner of his eye filming him with a camera. Who was that video for? The feds or whoever was pulling the strings? He'd contemplated Russia being behind this but why go to all the trouble of taking an American from his home in Colorado when Russia already had top-class hackers? He'd rubbed shoulders with them, even learned from them. No, what was the end game?

Blake swung his legs off the low bed and rolled his head around working out the tension. God, he hated the restraints. He couldn't scratch his back without getting up and rubbing against the bedpost. He just wanted to…

Footsteps approaching.

A hard bolt pulling back.

The door swung open and in stepped the doctor, and one of his captors. The doctor was told to wait by the door while his restraints were cut. On both occasions prior to that there had been two of them, one blocking the door while the other dealt with his restraints, but not this time. This was it. Now or never.

Blake gave a nod to the doctor and she lowered her chin — shame? Guilt? Fear? It was hard to know what was going through her mind, as they wouldn't let him talk to her other than to describe what pain he was in.

After getting free, he rubbed his wrists and the doctor

stepped forward and placed a bag down. "How are you feeling?" she asked, reaching into her bag and retrieving new bandages, and several devices she used to check his pulse, temperature and look in his eyes and ears.

"Better," he replied, his eyes darting to the door for a second.

As the doc began checking his vitals he sized up his captor. Unlike the other two, this one had an average build, no more than his. He wore a dark jacket, jeans, black boots and that mask, always that damn mask. Holstered at his hip was a Glock. He stood with his arms folded staring at him. "Though I did notice some blood in my urine," he said.

"When?"

"Yesterday."

"Why didn't you tell me?"

"It was after you left," Blake said.

There was no problem with his urine but he needed a reason that might require real medical attention, something beyond his prison. But it didn't work.

"I'll need you to go again, so I can see," she said.

The doc turned and told the guy what needed to be done and he told her to wait outside. She exited and Blake pulled out the steel bedpan they'd given him.

"You think I can get some privacy?"

Any time before that they'd stepped out but not now.

"Just go."

He shook his head and turned around and unzipped.

A few seconds, a trickle and then he filled the bedpan. Once he was done, he zipped up and picked up the bedpan but before he turned around he crouched over and began to groan as if he was in pain. Out the corner of his eye he saw the guy approach, walking straight into what he wanted. Blake spun around and struck him with the pan as hard as he could. Piss went all over him as the guy buckled.

A detonation of pure will to survive and Blake burst into action leaping around him and heading for the door. He swung it open to the surprise of the doctor and dashed down the steel corridor. *Where the hell am I?*

Angry yells echoed, his captor was now in pursuit.

Blake raced down the corridor until he came to a steel ladder fixed to the wall, he scaled up it with all the ease of a monkey, adrenaline pushing him on.

It took him up to another level, and into a room full of chairs, a TV and a table. He sprinted down the corridor to the next ladder and went up multiple floors, blasting through openings until he pulled back a steel door and wheeled out into the light of day.

Daylight stung his eyes.

Hours, days of being inside with nothing more than a light bulb had taken its toll. Without stopping to take in his surroundings, he wheeled around and reached for a railing and ascended steps.

There he found himself on a steel platform with a huge H at the center of it.

He spun around, 360 degrees, and took in the sight of the ocean. Nothing but water for miles. He spotted a few boats on the horizon, and what may have been land but it was too far away, nothing but a speck in the distance.

Blake considered jumping for a second but stopped short of the edge.

If the drop didn't kill him, the frigid waters would.

Within seconds his captors appeared, out of breath and brandishing handguns.

Though now there weren't three, there was a fourth. One of them extended their arms outward.

"It's the North Sea, there's nowhere to go," a familiar voice said. "You are the guest of the Principality of Sealand." He'd heard of it before. A tiny speck, seven miles off the east coast of the United Kingdom, the sea fort was grounded in international waters — a tiny nation unto its own. It had been constructed during the Second World War as a means of protecting England.

Blake stared back at them, overwhelmed. "I've given you everything you want."

"Not everything. There is still one more thing to be done, Blake."

"I just want to see my son."

"And you will."

The voice was so familiar.

"Who are you?"

The man stopped walking towards him and lifted his mask.

Blake squinted. "You?"

Chapter 1

10 Days into Blackout

Breckenridge, Colorado

Sam wiped beads of sweat from his brow after attaching another solar panel to the roof of Helen's house. He glanced out across the city of Breckenridge and felt a familiar sense of home. Although it varied each year, the weather was mild for October. They still hadn't had a dusting of snow but many of the aspens surrounding the town had turned golden making the entire Colorado landscape look like it had been set on fire.

Unlike Oneida, which had fallen hard and fast, the law enforcement of Breckenridge had maintained order, at least according to Richard. A city hall meeting was fast approaching and he planned on attending if only to find out the truth. People didn't mince words and if trouble was brewing he'd soon know.

According to Richard, the mountain town was

functioning, citizens were behaving and he didn't foresee that changing despite news of dwindling resources.

He wasn't fooling anyone, certainly not Sam.

As he made his way down the ladder at the side of Helen's house, he thought back to the years when things were good between them. She'd been like a pillar in his life, the one sure thing that kept him grounded. So much had changed.

It had been three days since they'd moved out of Richard's home on Iron Mask Road. What was meant to be only a one-night stay was drawn out into several days at the request of her grandfather. Of course he stated his reasons: safety, desire to be with Anna, and being one of only a few people with a working generator. Although Sam knew it was just another means of controlling the situation, he went along with it out of respect for his daughter but that all changed the morning Anna decided to return home.

His mind drifted.

Sam woke early that morning and for a moment he

thought he'd be the first to rise until he heard conversation downstairs. It didn't take long to recognize Richard's and Anna's voices.

"I don't understand, Anna. We have everything we need here — plenty of space, a good neighborhood, and a generator. There's no need to go home."

"I appreciate it, grandfather, but I think I'm ready. Besides, it's not fair on you."

"I told you I'm fine with them staying. Sure, Sam should consider moving on but the rest, they are more than welcome."

"I can't believe you just said that."

"What?" he replied so innocently.

"Don't play the ignorance card. You know."

Sam pulled back the covers and made his way over to the landing to hear more.

"Look, I appreciate him bringing you back but it doesn't change anything. This is where you belong and he has a home elsewhere. Your mother was clear about that."

"Don't bring her into it."

"Anna, I was there before she went in. I heard what she told me."

"You know what, I don't care. I'm heading out today. It's my life, it's my decision. Besides, I'll only be around the corner."

"It's not safe."

"It's not any safer here. In fact, if it weren't for my father I wouldn't be here now. I'm going to ask him to stick around. If you have a problem with that, speak to him."

Sam made his way down as they continued talking.

"Hold up, Anna. What are you going to do about a generator?"

"I'll figure it out."

"Security?"

"I'll figure it out."

"See, this is what I'm on about. You're still a child."

"I'm nineteen years of age."

"And now your mother is gone, I'm responsible for you. You're to stay here. If there is anything you want, we can go get it but there is no point in you heading back to the house.

It will only make you sad."

"You're not my mother. And you don't dictate what I do."

"Okay then, how are you going to feed yourself? You got a job?"

"How is anyone in this town going to feed themselves? Wake up. Have you not seen it out there?"

"The town is functioning fine. It'll only be a matter of days and the power will be back up and running, and then—"

"You are dreaming," Anna said. "You didn't see what I did out on the road. There are towns that have fallen. People have turned on each other."

"Absurd. It's only been ten days. There have been power outages across this country longer than that."

"But I think you're forgetting a very significant point in all of this."

"Yeah, what?" Richard asked.

"Those were in one area. One area. People outside of that gave assistance to get them through it. This is across the entire United States. It may very well be global. Every city, every

town and hamlet has been affected. Roads are clogged with vehicles. Transportation in the sky has been affected. Unless the government can reverse whatever has been done to the grid, no aid is coming, grandfather."

"I knew it. I knew this would happen. This is exactly why I didn't want your mother letting him near you. Your father has got into your head and filled it with fear-based, illogical nonsense."

Sam walked into the kitchen. Richard was standing close to Anna with both hands on her arms as if he was trying to prevent her from walking away.

"It's not nonsense, Richard, and I didn't say anything to her. Anna's seen it for herself. The problem here is you haven't but you will. Give it some time and Breckenridge will break."

Richard released his grip. "I won't have you polluting her mind."

"He's not," Anna said. "Please, grandfather, you don't understand."

"I understand very well," he said turning around to face

Anna. "I understand that he walked out many years ago and now he thinks he can come back and call the shots. Well you can't." Richard faced Sam from across the room. "I will not have you twisting the situation." He walked over to a drawer and pulled out a checkbook and pen. "So tell me, how much is it going to cost to have you leave?"

"Leave?" Sam replied.

"I want you gone today. Out of this house, out of Breckenridge."

"Grandfather," Anna raised her voice in protest.

Richard ignored her and walked over and scribbled into his checkbook before ripping off a sheet and handing it to him. "How's ten thousand dollars sound?"

Sam took it out of his hand and looked at it.

"Not enough?" Richard asked. "Okay, twenty thousand."

Sam shook his head and ripped up the check and tossed the pieces on the ground.

"I don't want your money."

"Then what do you want, huh?"

"I'm here because of Anna."

Richard stabbed his finger at him. "No! What's done is done. You made the decision to no longer be part of this family a long time ago."

"You know that's bullshit," Sam shot back. "If it wasn't for you I would still be here. You never once gave my relationship with Helen a chance."

"Don't you mean if it wasn't for you, cheating on my daughter?"

"She was just a friend, and I didn't do anything."

"That's not what the photos and video show."

Sam took a step forward and Richard backed up pointing his finger. "I would think very carefully about what you do next."

Anna was quick to jump between them.

"Please," she pleaded with them.

"Oh, don't worry. I'm not going to waste my time on you." Sam gave him a hard look. "I'll leave your house but not the town, not until Anna says so."

Richard looked at Anna and her eyes bounced between them.

"Anna?" Richard asked expecting her to make a decision.

"We're heading out this morning," she said.

"Anna!"

"I'm not doing this, grandfather."

They'd made so much noise that Mason and Chase had come down to find out what was going on. "Sam?" Mason asked as Anna walked past Sam leaving both of them standing there staring at each other.

Sam turned and patted him on the shoulder. "We're leaving this morning. Get your things together."

He snapped back into the present at the sound of banging.

Dropping to the ground, he turned to see Mason hammering No Trespassing signs around the 1.7-acre property. Helen's home was a gorgeous, custom log cabin bordering open space and Nordic trails. It was perched near Cucumber Gulch and looked directly at the Tenmile Range. Covering almost 6,000 square feet, the four-bedroom home was designed with timber trusses, handcrafted stone and the best material money could buy.

Of course, Richard wouldn't have expected her to live in anything less. The purchase of the property had been a cause of several arguments. Sam wanted a modest home in one of the many good neighborhoods in town among the rest of the hard-working folks of Breckenridge, but oh no, Richard wouldn't have that. It was all about appearances. It would reflect poorly upon him to have his family rubbing shoulders with blue collar. Helen stood by Sam even though he knew she wanted to live in the wealthier neighborhood. Who wouldn't? So instead of backing off and allowing them to forge their own way, Richard went behind Sam's back while he was overseas. He'd paid a designer to build a home and then he gave it as a gift to his daughter on her birthday.

What was Helen meant to do?

Sam was furious. But that was always Richard's way. He was a master manipulator. He knew she wouldn't turn it down. He rolled out the red carpet and gave her a tour of the place on her birthday. Richard even had the front porch wrapped with a red bow. It was sickening. And if that wasn't enough, he made sure that it was within walking distance of his home. Peerless Drive was just around the corner from Iron Mask Drive.

It was a slap in the face.

By the time Sam returned from the operation in Iraq, Helen had already moved in and got the baby bedroom set up for the birth of Anna. Richard couldn't have timed it any better.

That was one of many actions he took to shape the course of their life in the town, Eric Porter was another but that would come later.

"How are we doing?" Sam asked Mason.

He wiped away sweat and exhaled. "That's the last one in. You think these are really going to make much difference?"

"Any deterrent is better than no deterrent."

Mason leaned against a shovel and jammed a cigarette into his mouth. "You know, I've been doing a lot of thinking since losing Lisa."

"You want to return to Boston?" Sam asked.

"No. There's nothing for me there, besides…" He gazed around. "This town seems to be holding up okay."

"For now," Sam said looking back at the house. He noticed Anna in the window talking with Amanda.

Mason blew out smoke. "So when the power comes back on — what then?"

"What do you mean?" Sam asked.

"Will you stay?"

Sam hadn't given much thought to it. Originally the plan was to head out to Boston, reconnect with Anna, bring her back to Breckenridge and spend one more week there before returning to California but that was before the fall. He'd spent the better part of the last eleven years with his nose buried in military operations. While it had contributed to the loss of his marriage, it had saved him from losing his mind in some ways. Having something to funnel his anger and bitterness into had allowed him to keep his head above water, but now that was his past, nothing more than a line on a résumé. He looked back at Anna and thought of all the years he'd missed out on; the birthdays, the Christmases, the school years, he wasn't sure what he could offer her now but as long as she wanted him around and the situation didn't change he would remain here.

"To be honest, Mason, I'm just taking it day by day. Feeling my way out. This is all new to me."

Mason sniffed hard. "So what else do you want done?"

"What did you do with the solar pathway lights?" Sam asked.

"They're out back."

"Good. We'll bring those in tonight."

"Inside?"

"They might not give off a lot of light but as long as they are charged by the sun in the day they'll provide some illumination through the night. Saves us having to use gas in the generator. Which reminds me, how much gas do we have left?"

"We are scraping the bottom of the canister."

"What about the car?"

"Already drained it. By the way that was real nice of

Richard to get us a generator."

Sam snorted. "Yeah, real nice. Where's Chase?"

"I have him collecting water from the creek. He's set up barrels to collect rain water beneath the gutters, and I told him to position a few in the woods. Hopefully that should keep him busy for a while."

While they were talking, Anna and Amanda emerged from the garage with two bicycles. "Hey," Anna said. "I'm taking Amanda into town, show her around and see if we can help at the school."

Sam frowned. "At the school?"

"It's being used as an emergency shelter. I figure they could use a hand."

Sam thumbed over his shoulder. "But we have a lot to do around here."

She gave a broad smile. "We've already done it."

"The kick plate on the doors?"

"Installed."

"The 2 x 4 barricade?"

"In place. I'm way ahead of you."

"I don't see the window bars."

"We'll add them later," Anna said. "Dad, you worry too much."

"And you don't worry enough. Are you carrying?"

Anna lifted her top to show him the holstered Glock.

Sam was reluctant to let her go but he didn't want to be overbearing and controlling like her grandfather. At the end of the day she was nineteen, and she'd proven she could handle stress, and from what he'd seen of the town over the past few days, there was a strong show of police presence patrolling. "All right but just don't be too long, okay?"

He glanced at Amanda. Richard had got both Anna and her new clothes. She was now dressed in a pair of tight jeans, a white sweater, and had her dark hair pinned back. They hadn't spoken much since they'd arrived. Finding her fiancé dead had traumatized her, even more so than Mason losing Lisa. His reaction was to become withdrawn and quiet for several days then he seemed to snap out of it. Some might have thought it was odd but everyone processed death in different ways and Sam figured Amanda would eventually come around.

They gave a wave and rode off down the driveway disappearing behind the pines. Mason patted him on the arm. "Ah, she'll be fine. You've got a strong kid there. You should have seen the way she handled herself that day at the golf and country club. I swear she takes after her father."

Sam smiled and was about to get back to securing the property when he heard the crunch of tires on the gravel driveway. He cast a glance over his shoulder and saw a police vehicle pull in.

"Heads up," Mason said resting on his shovel.

A silver Chevy SUV with a blue stripe down the side rolled in. Sam instantly spotted Richard inside and sighed. He knew it was only a matter of time before he pulled some strings and tried to get Sam into trouble. The engine shut off and Richard and an officer got out.

"Whatever he's told you, officer, don't believe him. We've not done anything wrong."

Richard smiled, and the officer chuckled.

"You're not in any trouble," Richard said. "I just wanted to introduce you to Chief James Sanchez."

Sanchez was middle aged, with silver flecks in his hair, tanned, sporting a goatee and a bit of a paunch.

"Sam. Pleased to meet you."

Sam extended a hand and greeted him. "Likewise."

He had a firm handshake. Sam sized him up.

"Heard you had a long trip from Boston."

"That's right. So what can I do for you?"

"It's actually what you can do for the town," Sanchez said. "Richard here was telling me about your military background. He says you're planning on staying. Is that right?"

Sam nodded and glanced at Richard who shifted uncomfortably.

"Well, I'll cut to it. Obviously you are aware of the situation we're in. While the community is doing a great job of helping one another through this time, there has been an increase in theft and a couple of women have been attacked in their homes at night."

"And?" Sam asked.

"Our officers can only handle so much. With the curfew in place, and the need for more officers on the street, we've been seeking out anyone who has military background to assist. Richard here said you had. I thought you might be interested in helping."

Sam's gaze bounced between the two of them.

"Not sure I can help you there," Sam replied almost immediately.

"Huh. That's unfortunate." Sanchez turned to Richard. Richard put up a finger and stepped forward placing a hand around Sam's shoulder and urged him to walk with him. Sam shrugged his arm off. He didn't want him thinking he liked him. Richard had this way about him whereby he would make a person feel smaller than him, less important even.

"Look, Sam, I know we got off on the wrong foot but—"

"What's your angle?"

"My what?" Richard asked, his brow furrowing.

"C'mon, Richard, you always have a reason behind what you're doing."

"I don't have an angle. We have a need. If you are staying, then the situation here in the town affects you and Anna. Chief Sanchez brought up the need for more people helping in our meeting this morning. I recommended you. Is there a problem with that?"

"The problem is with you overstepping the line."

"The line?"

"Since I've known you, you have never asked. You push and pull. Then you stand there baffled as to why I resist."

He studied Sam, nodding ever so slightly.

"If you're not interested that's fine. But if those lights come back on, who knows, maybe this would give you a foot in with the department. A man of your skills — it can't be easy finding work now you're out of the military."

Sam scoffed. "So I'm to believe you want me here.

Working under your nose? C'mon. I'm not a fool."

"It's just an offer. Anyone who works for the department will receive more than their share of supplies. If you want to make this about you and me, fine, but I'm thinking about Anna here." He looked at the house. "If you're going to live in my house," he looked back at Sam, "I make the rules."

Sam ran a hand over his chin. "Your house?"

"Well I gave it as a gift."

"That's right. You did." Sam rolled his bottom lip in. "Which means it's no longer yours. It's Anna's."

Richard narrowed his eyes and then looked back at the chief who was now speaking with Mason. Sam could just make out bits and pieces of their conversation — something to do with the state of the town and trouble.

"Listen, whatever issues you and I have, this situation is bigger than that. We're not asking for a yes today. Chew it over and let me know."

"Let you know," Sam said, making it clear that he was stating he was the deciding factor in what happened in the town.

"Yeah. Me."

"But you're not mayor anymore, Richard."

"Oh, I must have forgot to tell you. I was reinstated. Our last one flew the nest."

Sam stood there dumbfounded, his eyes narrowed ever so slightly.

"Yeah." Richard put his hands on his hips and breathed in the crisp morning air. "It's good to be back at the helm." He looked back at Sam again as if hoping to get a reaction out of him. "Well you think about it."

"Yeah, I will."

As he went to walk away, Richard looked back.

"Who knows… would it be so strange if through all this we became friends?"

"Yes it would," Sam said. Richard grinned and walked back. The chief waved and Sam watched them get back into the SUV and drive off. Mason walked over with the shovel in hand.

"Is it me, or is there something about that guy that

doesn't feel right?"

Sam patted him on the back. "Welcome to Breckenridge."

Chapter 2

It was a good thirty-minute ride to Summit High School. The mammoth school was sandwiched between Frisco and Breckenridge. It was the largest school in the area and with a steady influx from both communities, it's size was perfect for an emergency shelter.

Anna and Amanda rode side by side on North Park Avenue. On either side of them were evergreen trees and a stunning view of the mountains. A cool breeze made the branches sway. Several vehicles whipped by them and for the first time Anna got a better look at what was being done in the community. For the most part the roads were clear, except in a few areas. Police had set up temporary checkpoints at the side of the road and were involved in clearing vehicles.

"So where are your parents, Amanda?" Anna asked casting a sideways glance at her.

"My mother lives in Florida, and my father left when I

was young. I have no idea where he is."

"How long were you living in Oneida?"

"Seven years. I landed a job at the local hospital. That's where I met David."

Anna nodded. She knew it was still a sensitive topic. She didn't want to pry and thankfully she didn't have to, Amanda opened up to her. It had been the first time since meeting her that she'd really had the chance to chat.

"Yeah, March 2011, he came into the emergency department with a broken arm." She smiled. "I can still see the look on his face."

Anna shifted down a few gears and the chain clattered.

"I'm curious. What made you come with us?"

"You know, in the heat of the moment I didn't think about it. But I guess…" Amanda trailed off. "I never really had a relationship with my mother. You could say it was strained. Now had David still been alive we would have probably been in Syracuse right now."

"We drove right by there. You know we could have dropped you off."

Amanda nodded. "I couldn't have done that. I only met his family once. Besides, I can't go back to Oneida, not until things get better. That town is out of control. Truthfully, I'm surprised this place isn't the same way."

Anna kept a steady rhythm as she pedaled. Amanda was right. It was strange to see how things were being handled in the town. Then again, not all communities would spiral out of control in the first two weeks even with zero aid from surrounding towns. Breckenridge had always been known as a friendly town where folks helped each other out. It was the reason she wanted to get out of the house to help at the emergency shelter. That, and she was going stir crazy being at the house.

"How are you coping?" Amanda asked.

"It's hard."

"It is," Amanda replied. "And yet you seem to be doing better than me."

It was nice to find someone who she had something in common with, even if it was something as morbid as the death of a loved one. Having been sent away to a private school when she was young, Anna had learned not to wear her feelings on her sleeve but bury them instead. Those that were seen as weak were often preyed upon. She'd figured that out pretty quickly.

"Believe me. I'm not," Anna said.

"What about your father, Sam? What's his deal?"

"What do you mean?"

"I get a sense that you two don't get along very well, or you're not tight with him."

"He's been out of my life since I was eight."

"Oh," she said. "Sorry."

"It's okay." Anna was quick to change the subject. Up ahead the road was blocked with police vehicles that had pulled over a large military style truck. They had the occupants out and pushed up against the side and weapons were drawn. Slowing down, she eyed Highlands Drive off to her right. "Here, let's go this way. I know a shortcut."

They veered off the main stretch and continued heading north, parallel to Highway 9. They hadn't made it two miles down the road when they saw a group of four young adults crowding near the edge of the road. They were dressed in dirt-bike gear and looked as if they had stopped to help someone. As they got closer, Anna noticed the person they were crowding wasn't being helped, it was an older man and they were robbing him. He was clinging to two gasoline cans and one of the guys was trying to pull it away, while another pulled out a baseball bat that he had attached to his back and started hitting the man across the back.

The old guy curled into a ball.

Anna put her hand out and touched Amanda's arm.

They slowed and came to a stop.

Before they had a chance to decide what to do, two of the bikers saw them. Anna quickly turned her bike around and made a break for it. Dirt bikes roared to life and Anna shouted, "This way." She went off road, zipping down a steep hill that fed into a long stretch of road. She glanced back and saw two Kawasaki bikes soar over the rise. Why the hell were they chasing them? They didn't have anything. In the heat of the moment Anna completely forgot she was carrying a Glock. She pedaled as fast as she could to try and put distance between them but they were closing in. Her heart caught in her chest. Her first instinct was to head for the nearest house. The homes were spread out before them, set back against a hilly landscape. Her knuckles went white from gripping the handlebars so tight, and her cheeks flushed red from the cold. Their bikes came screeching around a bend and Anna veered into a driveway. As soon as she reached the entranceway, she jumped off not even hitting the brakes and raced towards the door with Amanda not far behind.

Frantically Anna banged on the door, and yelled for help, her fear and natural survival instincts kicking in.

No one answered.

"Come on!" she cried out looking over her shoulder.

Amanda dropped her bike and hurried over and began beating on the door just as the two dirt bikes rumbled into the driveway. They stopped just short of their bikes and the drivers cut the engines and got off. They didn't remove their helmets but she could tell they were male by the muffled voices. Both found the whole event amusing.

One of them slid out a baseball bat attached to his back and twirled it around.

"What do we have here?"

"Ladies," the other said.

"Go away!" Amanda yelled putting herself in front of Anna because she was older.

The guy rolled the bat in his hand. "Or what?"

"The cops are not far from here."

"No they're not, and?"

It didn't seem to faze them. As Anna moved to get around Amanda she felt the weight of the Glock at her side. She pulled up her top and pulled the gun. Immediately she felt a surge of confidence as she stretched it out.

"Get the hell out of here! Or I swear I will…"

The two guys stopped moving towards them and glanced at each other, a look of shock, maybe skepticism on their faces. She could tell they were trying to determine if it was real or not.

"Why do I get the sense that gun isn't loaded?" one of them said.

Without hesitation, she fired a round near his foot and they immediately backed up with their hands out. "Okay, okay. We're gone."

Now she was the one moving forward. Anna stepped out from underneath the porch raking the gun between them. "Get out of here. Now!"

The two guys backed up quickly, hopped on their bikes, brought them to life and tore away leaving a plume of dust in their wake. Anna and Amanda remained there for a few minutes until they felt it was safe to move on.

They pushed their bicycles out of the driveway and looked off down the road. Besides a nearby neighbor who'd come out to see what all the noise was about, no one was there. They were gone.

Amanda climbed onto her seat. "Let's go before they return."

"I doubt they will." Anna stared off down the road.

She could have continued on but the thought of that man lying on the road ate away at her.

"Anna?" Amanda said trying to get her attention

"We should go back," Anna said.

"What? Are you serious?"

"You saw what they were doing to him."

Amanda brought her bicycle around and came over. "Look, I would help but let's just tell the police and let them deal with it."

"You saw how full their hands were. They're probably dealing with multiple incidents like this. No, we should go back."

Amanda sighed, and then nodded. It didn't take them more than five minutes to retrace their steps. When they reached the section of road on Highland Drive the man was still there, curled up in a ball. The bikers were gone. They looked both ways and stood there for a minute or two to make sure the coast was clear before they made their way over. Anna slid off her bike and hurried over. The guy moaned, and it looked as if his head was bleeding. There was a large patch of blood on the ground near him, droplets dripped from his head.

"Hey mister," Anna said getting close.

The man squirmed and cowered back.

"It's okay. I'm not going to harm you. Those men are gone."

The man was in his early sixties with a sharp nose, sunken eyes and silver hair. He was wearing a thick jacket and had dark jeans on with large rain boots. His knuckles were red, and slightly torn as if he'd fought back.

"Amanda, give me a hand."

She got off her bike and cautiously approached.

"You're a doctor, right?" Anna said.

"No, just a nurse."

"We need to get him to the hospital. Do you think you can stay with him while I ride back to the police blockade and alert them?"

"Stay here alone?"

Anna pulled out the gun and handed it to her.

Amanda backed away. Fear dominated her mind just

like it had in Oneida. It was to be expected. She'd witnessed close up and personal the horrors of a town that turned against each other. She'd seen how things could go wrong in a matter of seconds.

"Fine. I'll stay here," Anna said. "You ride back."

"But what if those guys are farther down the road?"

Her brow furrowed. "Amanda, he's bleeding out. He needs helps. We certainly can't place him on the back of our bikes." Anna felt like she was talking to a teenager but it was clear Amanda was still traumatized by the events in Oneida. It wasn't a matter of being strong minded or fearless, Anna was neither. She was just as scared but she wasn't going to let it paralyze her. She looked at Amanda assuming she would snap out of whatever state she was in but it didn't appear she would.

"Look, one of us needs to go for help." Anna looked off down the road. "A friend of my mom lives on this road." She got up and grabbed her bike. "Stay with him, I'll be right back."

"Anna. You can't expect me to—"

"Please."

Anna took off pedaling as fast as she could. She didn't want to leave her behind but one of them needed to make a decision and Amanda clearly wasn't in her right frame of mind.

It had been a while since she'd spoken with or seen Eric Porter.

Not long after her father had left Breckenridge, he'd shown up, comforting her mother and running a few errands. From the little she'd managed to glean from her mother over the years, he was just a friend, a good friend but nothing more. She had a sense the feeling wasn't mutual.

Anna recalled visiting him at Thanksgiving a couple of years back when she'd returned home. Her grandfather was there and her mother had made a big thing about it and said that he didn't have anyone to spend Thanksgiving with so that's why they were joining him, but she wasn't dumb. She knew their friendship had progressed. With her father out of the picture it wasn't uncommon for her mother to mention Eric in their conversations on the phone. While she never admitted that they were dating, Anna kind of knew they were spending time together. In some ways she resented it and in other ways she appreciated Eric being there for her mother. It couldn't have been easy.

"Now which house was it?" she muttered to herself scanning the homes as she went by. She must have gone by at least ten homes before she spotted the road sign, and a red mailbox. The memory of that night came back to her. Anna swerved into his driveway. *Please, be home; please be home,* she thought as she made her way up to the house. As she came around a cluster of trees, there was her grandfather's 1948 Chevrolet 3100 pickup. She'd recognize that anywhere. When she was young her grandfather would take her out to the garage and let her sit in his multiple classic cars. He would rattle on about different models he owned and ones he wanted to collect. Back then she thought he was kind of cool but over time she came to see how controlling he was.

Ditching her bike by the door she knocked and called out to him.

"Eric. It's Anna."

She cupped hands over her eyes and peered through a window. As soon as she saw him in the kitchen she breathed a sigh of relief. He turned, smiled and made his way down. The door swung open and before he could greet her she pointed back to the road. "There's a guy injured. I need your help."

Without waiting for a yes, she grabbed up her bicycle.

"Hold on, Anna, we'll throw it in the back."

He came out and lifted it into the rear and went and got his keys for the truck. Within minutes they peeled out of his driveway heading back to the spot.

"Who is it?" Eric asked, as the truck rumbled down the road.

"Not sure. We ran into a group of young guys on dirt bikes. They gave him a beating and stole gasoline from him and took off."

"Bastards."

As they came over a rise Anna spotted Amanda sitting beside the guy with her hand on his head. He was still curled up in a fetal position, like an injured animal beside the road; it was the most pitiful sight she'd ever witnessed.

"Ah damn, that's Gene Landers."

Anna squinted. "You know him?"

"Not personally but I know his son. They own a hardware store in town."

He veered the truck to the hard shoulder.

"How long has he been here?"

"Ten minutes, maybe longer."

Eric hurried over and assessed his situation. He checked him out before asking for help. "C'mon, give me a hand."

Gene groaned as they hauled him up and carried him to the truck. Amanda supported him from the other side as they slipped him into the back. Amanda hopped in the rear and Eric returned to grab up her bicycle. Within minutes they were driving away from the scene.

"When did you get back?" Eric asked.

Anna looked over her shoulder and checked on Amanda in the back, she was stroking the guy's head and holding a piece of rag that Eric had given her to stop the bleeding.

"About five days ago. We were at my grandfather's."

"How did you get back?"

"My father."

Eric's expression changed. "Is he still here?"

She nodded.

Eric returned to looking at the road ahead, a look of concern spread on his face. "I'm sorry about your mother, Anna. She was a good woman."

Anna's chin dropped a little, and she nodded.

"Are you planning on staying?" he asked.

"Yeah. For now, I guess. It's pretty bad out there."

"What was Boston like?"

She shrugged. "We didn't stay there long enough to see it come apart but we traveled through plenty of towns that were in a worse state than Breckenridge."

"Yeah, well we have your grandfather to thank for that.

If he hadn't paid for all those generators, I'm sure we'd have been in a worse state than we are."

Eric eyed his rearview mirror. "Who's the woman?"

Anna shifted and looked back. "Amanda Baker. She lost her fiancé in Oneida."

He nodded. "Where are you heading?"

"To Summit High School to help out."

Eric smiled. "Just like your mother."

"What do you mean?"

"I'm pretty sure she would be out there now if she had made it." He breathed in deeply. "Well, I'll drop you guys off on the way and make sure Gene gets the medical attention he needs." He glanced at Anna again. "It's really good to see you home, Anna."

Anna looked at him and gave a strained smile.

Chapter 3

The cinch of his hood was loosened, and a meaty hand pulled it off. Someone stepped back behind him. Blake squinted hard as the world snapped into view. Sunlight flooded in through a window, dust drifted in the air and questions bombarded his mind. *Where am I now?* He recalled a brief conversation with Michael Thorn, otherwise known as Solo in the world of hackers, and then he remembered being restrained and injected, after that it was a blur.

Within seconds he got his answer.

He was home.

In his apartment in Frisco, Colorado.

It was in his kitchen. He squinted at the figures before him. It took but a second to recognize who they were — Thorn, and his thirteen-year-old son Aidan.

"Aidan."

"Dad."

"Did they do anything to you?"

He shook his head.

Blake's eyes flitted to Thorn who was tucking into a bowl of pasta.

"How's it feel to be home, Blake?"

"What are you doing?" He struggled to move because his wrists and feet were bound to a chair. Thorn sat across from him. He had a shaved head, and was wearing a jean jacket and V-neck shirt.

He stopped eating and continued talking. "It's a nice place you've got here. Must have cost you a fortune. But I expect it was nothing with that security consulting business of yours, huh?" He stabbed his butter knife at him and cut into a roll before taking a second to butter it. "How long has it been since we last saw each other?"

"Let my kid go. He's done nothing."

"Settle down, Blake. I'm not gonna harm him."

"I don't believe you." He gritted his teeth. "Why did you kill my wife?"

Thorn pulled a face and stopped chewing.

"Correction. You killed her. You see, had you done what you were asked, she would have been returned home and Aidan here would have been none the wiser. Hell, we'd even left him a note." He wagged his knife in the air and squinted. "You know, I really thought she'd be the one to tip you over the edge but obviously not."

Blake's nostrils flared. He so badly wanted to reach across the desk and wring his neck. He and Thorn went way back. They'd had met through a hacking forum back in the early '90s not long before Blake was imprisoned. They'd worked on a number of projects together and created worms that could infect systems. Back then they were friends, close partners in a new age of information and technology. They were the ones pushing the envelope of what could be achieved long before hacking groups like Anonymous formed.

"Why are you doing this?"

Thorn continued eating. Blake looked around the room and saw several others. At a rough head count there looked to be around ten. None of them were wearing masks now. He only recognized a few faces, hackers from years gone by, those who had gone over the edge: Dmitry Petrov, responsible for multiple DDoS attacks was sentenced to a year in federal prison back in early 2000. Niles Black, sentenced to four years behind bars for publishing credit card information and his involvement in the Stratfor hack. And then there was Hector Richardson, who had served three years for telecommunications fraud. They stared back at him but never said a word.

"Isn't it obvious?" Thorn said, shoveling away some more pasta.

"You want to get back at me."

He laughed and looked at the others. "Always about you, isn't it, Blake? The most famous hacker of our generation and you always think it's about you. Not this time." He stabbed a piece of pasta and brought it to his lips then paused. "Of course making that plea deal didn't do you any favors. You know, if it wasn't for you, they wouldn't have found me."

"I could say the same thing."

In his prime he was untouchable. The feds had no idea where he was until someone gave him up.

"Wasn't me. That was your own fault. Trusting people outside of our circle." He finished off his meal and reached for a glass of beer, took a sip and leaned back and glanced at Aidan.

"Did your old man ever tell you what he used to do?"

"I already know," Aidan said.

"Of course you do." He smirked and lit a cigarette and blew smoke out the corner of his mouth. "Humility was never your strong point, was it, Blake?" He nodded a few times before continuing. "Must have been nice only doing five years inside the pen. Me? They were looking at throwing me in for twenty. Had it not been for the help of Dmitry over here I would still be locked up."

"Where did you go?"

He stifled a laugh. "After I jumped bail I fled across the border to Canada then took a private plane to Moscow. Russia welcomed me with open arms. Can you imagine that? All these years our government has been painting them in a bad light but when it came down to letting me walk, or throwing away the key, well we all know what our government would have done."

"So you're working for the Russians now?"

"Me? Work for someone else?" He laughed. "Surely you know me better than that, Blake."

"So what is this? Some game you want to play with the government?"

He took a hard pull on his cigarette. "Game? Maybe. I mean it's been fun so far but like anything, the fun has to come to an end. We have one final piece of the puzzle to finish and then we'll be heading out."

"So why am I still alive?"

"I made a promise, didn't I? I said you would get to see your son and you have."

"What are you playing at, Thorn?"

Thorn wiped the corner of his lips with a napkin then got up from his seat and walked around the kitchen. He picked up a framed photo of Blake's family. It had been taken a few years back at one of Aidan's first martial arts tournaments. He'd been taking Taekwondo for four years and had already won several state competitions.

"Such a shame. She really was a pretty little thing. Tell me, Blake, where did you meet her? Giving one of your talks? Did she buy your book? Or stand in line to see the movie they based on you?" He grinned, shooting him a sideways glance. "That's right, I've been keeping close tabs on you. You get out and you're this unsung hero. Invited to speak at security consulting events, put up at fancy hotels and gifted with some of the wealthiest clients in the USA. Me? I've had to hide in the shadows for the past nine years. No longer welcome in my own country."

"Perhaps you shouldn't have jumped bail then."

Thorn smiled and glanced at him before putting the photo down.

"Cute." He returned to the table and drained the remainder of his drink. When he was done he sat back down. "You want to know my end game? Huh?"

Blake stared back at him.

"These past ten days have been good. Believe me, I

could leave the country in this state and be satisfied. Of course there would be a huge loss of life but wisdom tells me that right now we have some of the best minds in government working hard to get that grid back up again so I know it's only a matter of time before they figure it out and the lights come back on." He breathed in deeply and looked at the others. "Now I could wait for that or... I could do everyone a favor and bring it back up."

"Just like that?" Blake asked, slightly confused.

Thorn made a gesture to Dmitry. He pulled out a cell phone and handed it to him. Thorn looked back at Blake. "Oh the wonders of satellite," he said as if clarifying how it would work. He then glanced at his watch. "A couple more minutes and we should be good for testing this baby out, thanks to you. You see, as good as I am at hacking, you were always better, Blake. And you took every opportunity to make that clear to me."

"I was a different person back then."

He laughed. "Really? So am I expected to believe you're now a changed man?"

Blake didn't answer him.

Thorn looked at his wristwatch again. Thorn then got on the phone, dialed a number and brought it up to his lips. He walked off and mumbled a bit and then returned and handed the phone back, and slipped back into his chair.

"I don't get it."

"C'mon, Blake. Don't act ignorant. You know what we're gonna do. We talked about it, don't you remember?"

Blake stared back at him racking his mind for why he'd want the grid down, and why he would bring it back up again.

Because he didn't respond, Thorn filled in the gap. "Five letters, Blake. Silos."

Right then the reality of what he was doing sank in.

He shook his head. "No. You will kill millions."

Thorn sighed. "We really need to work on this communication. Correction. You will kill millions. Me? I will be long gone. Out of sight. Out of mind. Out of the country. But you…" He reached into his pocket and pulled out a small smartphone, swiped, tapped a few keys and played back a video of him bringing the grid down.

It was proof, damning evidence that… Blake gritted his teeth and lunged forward, shifting the chair ever so slightly towards him.

"You bastard!"

Thorn laughed. "Settle down, Blake. It's all good. You see, we're just resetting the world. Leveling the scales of justice. Bringing it back to the way it should be — free. Free from fear. Free from nuclear weapons. Free from tyranny and injustice. And having fun all at the same time. Right?" he said. "That's why we got into this, for the fun of it. Don't you remember telling me that?"

Blake chuckled. "You're an idiot. I can't hack into the silos or launch control centers. No one can. They are off the grid. They are self-contained with everything they need including diesel generators. They don't draw their power entirely from outside. So go ahead, bring up the power. You can't do shit!"

"Oh the power coming back on isn't for hacking into the launch control facilities. It's for this video of you to be distributed to the NSA. After that, it's going back down again. You see, for what we're about to do, we can't have prying eyes, and even though the grid is down, you're right… that emergency generator at the launch facilities in Wyoming will still be functioning." He paused and smiled. "Well, for now."

Silence stretched between them before Blake asked, "How? How are you going to do it?"

"Don't worry. Leave that to us. Though I would have thought someone like you would have been able to figure that out."

Suddenly, there was a surge of power. The lights blinked on, and the clock on his stove started flashing. Thorn gave a broad smile and waved his arm around.

"Look at that. Just like magic. I have to say, Blake. The work you did was spectacular. I couldn't have done better myself. Now it's set up like a light switch, we can shut it down, bring it up whenever we like." He looked up at the ceiling. "I wonder what the government would have paid us if we'd installed ransomware?" He paused for a second. "Ah, doesn't matter."

Thorn looked down at his phone and Dmitry brought over a laptop.

Thorn took his place at the table. "Now just a few small things to do and this file will be on its way and in the hands of the NSA in no time." He started tapping away at the keys and Blake looked over at his son. His pulse sped up as he began to connect the dots in his mind. The United States only operated 450 LGM Minuteman-III ICBM missiles at three silo locations in the west: Malmstrom Air Force Base in Montana, Minot AFB in North Dakota and F.E. Warren AFB in Wyoming and partially in Colorado. They had been developed as a deterrent back in the 1950s and were made active in 1962 at the height of the cold war to counterattack if the U.S. was attacked by the Soviet Union. The launch facilities still operated using outdated archaic technology from the 1960s and 8-inch floppy disks. According to the government it remained that way in order to protect them from being hacked but recent information had come to light to suggest that the launch control sites were still vulnerable to hacking through the HICS cable system or the silo radio receivers.

Thorn hit a final button and leaned back in his chair. "There we go. The file originating from your home, your computer, detailing exactly what you did. Of course we didn't show them everything. We can't have them bringing the grid back up again, can we?"

"You're going to launch the missiles at Russia, aren't you?"

He smiled. "Now you're catching on!"

Back when they were friends, young and full of ego, they'd chewed over the idea. He wasn't serious about it. It just posed a challenge. Could they do it?

Blake turned his head. "Dmitry."

Thorn snorted. "Oh don't look at him. He doesn't care. In fact it was his idea. I just wanted to bring the grid down and fuck with the system. Dmitry? Well, let's say

Russia hasn't exactly treated him well and so..."

He trailed off glancing at his watch again. "Any minute now." Thorn smiled. "Can you imagine the look on everyone's face across the country right now? The power is back up! I can almost hear them cheering. The sense of relief, and then..." He glanced back at his watch. Suddenly, the power went off again. "Oh dear. The power has gone out again. What a travesty."

"Thorn, don't do this. This won't just affect Russia. You'll start World War Three."

"I know. Isn't it beautiful?"

He was out of his mind. Thorn rocked back in his chair relishing the situation.

"You need the power off so they don't see you coming, don't you? You've got to do it manually. That's why you're back here."

Thorn pointed at him. "Nothing gets by you, does it, Blake? That's why I liked you. You were always one step ahead. It's a pity things turned out the way they did. If you'd just kept your mouth closed..."

Thorn shut off the computer and rose from the table.

"Do you know the government showed up on my family's doorstep? They hassled them so much — you know, wanting to know where I was that my mother had a stroke. I couldn't even make it back for her funeral."

Blake was at a loss for words.

Thorn breathed in deeply and picked up the empty bottle of beer and flipped it in the air, catching it by the neck. In one smooth move he smashed half of it on the table leaving a shard of jagged glass in his hand.

Without missing a beat he walked around the table and yanked Aidan's head back.

"Thorn, no. Kill me."

"Oh, I'm not going to kill you. I want you to suffer."

With that said he slid the glass across Aidan's throat.

Blake's scream caught in his throat as Thorn turned and walked out of the house leaving him bound to a chair watching his son bleed out.

Chapter 4

Chase waded ankle deep into the crystal waters of Cucumber Creek; found a deep spot of water and submerged a section of the green metal canister below the surface. He squinted into the bright morning sky and kept his eyes peeled for trouble. Although Breckenridge didn't appear to have stooped to the depths that Oneida had, he knew it only took a couple of bad apples. Cucumber Creek was a good couple of miles trek through the dense woodland that surrounded the Shock Hill neighborhood. He didn't like the idea of being out there with nothing more than a lever action .44 Winchester rifle. Even though Sam had taken him through a few drills and shown him how to use one, he still didn't feel comfortable. He considered himself a city boy; the idea of living off the grid and having to defend territory was foreign to him.

He scooped up the canister and was making his way

back to the rocky shore when he heard what sounded like dead branches breaking. His eyes flitted nervously to the left, and then the right, and his pulse sped up. Just as he exited the water two men emerged into the clearing carrying similar canisters to his. Fearful, he dropped his and yanked the rifle off his back.

Hands raised. "Whoa, it's okay, we're just here to collect some water," said a tall, burly fella with a dark beard. The other one was scrawny, and carrying two canisters.

"Sorry, can't be too careful," Chase said.

"I hear you. Did you see the power come back on?"

His brow pinched. "It came on?"

"For all of ten minutes then it shut off again."

A smile formed on his face. Maybe the government is close to fixing this shit storm.

"Yeah, maybe. Well I've got to get going." Chase quickly gathered up the other canister, gave a nod and darted into the woodland, looking over his shoulder every so often. Although they didn't attack, he didn't feel comfortable being out in the middle of nowhere under the current conditions.

As he was making his way back through the woods, he heard footsteps behind him again. This time when he turned he noticed the men were back and this time not carrying any of the canisters.

"Hey, hold up. You got a light?"

He backed up. "Don't smoke. Sorry."

"You from Shock Hill?"

"Not from the area. Just staying with some friends."

"Same here," the bearded guy said. "You driving?"

Chase shook his head. His nerves were on high alert.

"Damn, that's too bad. Was hoping to get a boost. You think you can give us a hand? Our vehicle broke down over on Ski Hill Road."

"Sorry, I really need to get back."

"It'll only take a minute. We just need an extra hand to push start it. Dang thing gave up the ghost."

"So why aren't you there?" Chase asked.

"Oh, right, yeah, well we'd come out to get water."

The two men kept moving forward. The other guy was rail thin, had sunken eyes and his hood up. He looked like a tweaker. He kept sniffing and his eyes darted nervously all around the woodland.

"Look man, I'd like to help but I have friends expecting me."

"C'mon. It's only ten minutes out of your day."

"Sorry."

"You're not exactly being very neighborly, are you?"

Chase left them behind and changed direction, crossing through a cluster of trees, across another small stream and up a steep slope. He glanced back and grimaced. The men were still following.

"Hey, hold up."

Chase turned and noticed the tweaker guy had disappeared. He scanned the trees but couldn't see him. The bearded one was still following and getting closer. It was clear how this was going to end. He dropped the water and pulled his rifle around.

"I told you. I can't help. Now fuck off!"

"Fuck off?" The guy stopped and shifted from one foot to the next. "Now that's not nice. We're out here trying to survive and ask for a little assistance and you act like a jackass."

Chase kept his rifle pointing at the man, while trying to get a bead on where the other one had gone. He hadn't seen him pass him but the woodland was dense and it wouldn't have taken much to disappear.

"Look. All we want is five minutes of your time."

"And I told you I can't."

"Have it your way then."

There was a rustle off to the left side of him, and he saw a blur of darkness dart out. Before he had a chance to fire a round, the second guy emerged, lunged forward and took him down with a tackle. As he hit the ground, his finger squeezed the trigger and the gun went off. A flock of birds broke from the trees and he heard boots running towards him.

Chase struggled beneath the tweaker's grasp. Close up he looked even more ugly than he had from a distance.

His attacker was trying to jam the rifle down on his neck. It was taking every ounce of strength to hold him at bay. For someone who had zero muscle, the guy certainly had some unusual strength. One glance into his eyes and Chase could tell he was high.

Before he could bounce him off, the bearded fella reached them and latched a hand around Chase's neck. "Now calm down. No one needs to die."

"What do you want?" Chase asked.

"Well let's start by letting that rifle go, shall we?"

"Can't do that. It's not mine," Chase said.

"Kid, is it worth losing your head?" the guy said withdrawing a handgun and pushing it against his temple. Chase didn't hesitate, he let go of the rifle and tweaker pulled it away, a look of glee on his face as if he'd won some competition. Next they started rooting through his pockets, emptying out several dollars onto the ground.

"What the hell?" Chase asked. "C'mon, man."

"You got keys to a house, a car?"

"No, I told you I'm not driving and I'm staying with

others."

"On Shock Hill. Those homes are worth something. How about you—"

"Let him go!" a familiar voice bellowed from behind them.

Both men looked up from their crouched position to see Mason and Sam nearby aiming their guns at them. "Asshole. Did you not hear him?" Sam asked, making his way over. He took their guns and had to kick the tweaker away as he obviously wasn't paying attention or was too high to understand.

The bearded fellow cowered back with his hands raised. "Hey man, it's cool. We're just..."

"Trying to rob him. Yeah, we see that," Mason said. "Now get out of here."

Sam gestured with a wave of his M4 for them to get going.

"Can we at least get our guns?"

"Are you joking?" Mason said as he pushed towards them in an intimidating manner. They scrambled back and turned and fled melting into the forest within seconds. Sam extended a hand and Chase clamped onto it. He hauled him up and patted him on the shoulder.

"Damn, I am glad to see you guys."

"Don't thank me, it was Mason who said we should come looking for you. What was taking you so long?"

"Uh, I don't know, maybe I got held up by two freaks."

"You left over two hours ago," Mason said.

Chase rose and brushed off the earth's grime. "I got a little lost."

"How can you get lost?" Mason said. "You only had to stick to the path."

"I must have got off the path."

Sam patted him on the back and they retrieved the canisters and made their way back to the house.

"What did they want?" Mason asked as they trudged through the woodland in silence.

"They were looking for keys to a truck or a house."

"You think it's wise that we let them go?" Mason asked

Sam.

"I'm not in the business of killing people without reason."

"They were holding a gun up to his head."

"And?"

Mason continued. "We should have taken them in. Handed them over to the cops."

Sam pushed through a large thicket of branches. "No doubt they have their hands already full. Besides, what are they going to do? Put everyone in jail? If this continues to go the way I think it will, those cells will be filled in no time and then what?"

They trudged back to the house. Golden leaves blew across the ground like tumbleweed.

"So why don't you take up Richard's offer?" Mason asked.

"Are you kidding me?" Sam replied casting him a serious look. "No, that man has only one intention and that is my downfall."

"Didn't seem that way. I chatted with Chief Sanchez.

He was pretty straight about the situation in Breckenridge. It's getting worse with each passing day. The nights are the hardest. They've already had multiple home invasions, and even a rape."

"Hold on a second," Chase said. "The chief of police was here?"

Mason nodded. "This morning."

"What did he want?"

"To bring on board Sam to help out."

Chase looked at him. "That's a good thing, right?"

"In any other town, yes. This one?" Sam shook his head. "It's just another one of Richard's mind games."

"You really dislike the man, don't you?" Mason said. "What's the deal between you and him? I know you said he accused you of cheating but you didn't, right? So why does he keep riding you over it?"

"Because he set me up."

"What?"

Sam groaned thinking about it again. He'd tried to forget but it was lingering there in the back of his mind like a bad dream. "I really don't want to go into it. We should just head back and continue getting the house prepared."

"Prepared for what?" Chase said. "You're acting like the whole town will go nuts."

Sam turned and latched onto him. "Chase. You nearly got your ass served to you back there. Had we not shown up, the wildlife would have been chewing on your ass for supper tonight. What happened today was just the beginning. I don't care what Richard says about this town, he's deluded. It will fall and when it does I intend to be ready."

"I've been thinking about that," Chase said. "I'm not sure I'm going to stay. The only reason I agreed to come along was because you mentioned you were heading back to California. But it sounds like you're going to be staying."

"My main priority is Anna's safety. If that means I have to stay, I will."

Chase nodded. "I'm not sure I want to."

"Chase, you think it's any better out there?"

"I didn't say it is but I have family out there. They'll be wondering where I am."

Sam nodded as they came out of the tree line and made their way across an open field at the back of the neighborhood. "If you have to leave, I understand."

"You think that's wise?" Mason chimed in. "I mean after what happened out there in the woods? You had a gun on you and it didn't work out well."

"I…" Chase went to say something but he didn't know what to say. Mason was right; he'd freeze out there. Fear had got the better of him and a lack of experience of being in that kind of situation didn't help. The city was full of danger and although he might be able to dodge some of it, this was all new to him. He wasn't skilled like Sam, and he didn't have the hunting experience of Mason.

"Don't worry, Chase. It happens to the best of people. You should have seen some of the guys in boot camp in their first week. Not everyone takes to guns. In time you'll become more comfortable with it. It'll soon feel natural like an extension of your own body."

Mason laughed. "It will if he shoots himself in the foot."

Chase scowled as they made their way around the house. No sooner had they arrived than Sam groaned. "C'mon man, what's he want now?"

Richard's vehicle was out front but there was no one there. They could hear two people arguing inside the house as they approached the door. As soon as they entered Richard turned his way. "There is he. Was it your idea to let her go out by herself?" he bellowed.

Sam put up a finger. "You might want to mind your tone."

"Mind my tone?"

Anna stepped out of the kitchen area into the hallway. "Grandfather, drop it."

"I will not." He charged toward Sam. "Do you know what happened?" Sam looked at him then at Anna. "She was almost attacked."

Sam frowned. "Anna?"

She waved him off. "We weren't attacked. We ran into a little trouble on the road but it wasn't anything we couldn't handle. I don't appreciate the way you made me look like a fool in front of all those people," she said to her grandfather. "I was there to help and dragging me out was humiliating."

"Humiliating is having you serving up food. None of my family is going to do that."

"Why? Because it's below us?" she asked.

He didn't answer that, instead he turned back to Sam.

"If you don't watch over her, I will."

"I'm not going back to your house," Anna said.

"Hold on a minute," Sam interjected. "You want to bring me up to speed on what is going on?"

Richard laughed. "Always the last to know. Tell me, where have you been?"

"He came to my aid," Chase said. "I was attacked out near the creek."

"Nonsense. This place is friendly."

Even Chase shook his head.

Sam jabbed his finger at the door. "Richard. I want you out of here now."

"I own this house."

"Out of here now!" Sam bellowed opening the door and thrusting a hand out to make it clear. Richard stormed outside but turned to have the last say.

"This is not over. If I catch my granddaughter out there by herself again, I will…"

Before he could spit the words out Sam slammed the door in his face. "God, he doesn't shut the hell up." He looked at Anna. "You okay?"

"I'm fine," she said before noticing a cut on Chase's forehead. "You want to fill me in on what happened?"

"Oh just a rumble in the woods, you know, the run-of-the-mill stuff that happens when the world goes to shit." Chase ambled into the living room and slumped down on the couch while Anna went to find some warm water and a first-aid kit to patch him up.

"Anna," Sam said catching up. "You not going to tell

me?"

"Depends, are you going to act like him?"

Sam raised an eyebrow.

She sighed and brought him up to speed. When she was done he stood there staring at her. What occurred wasn't what bothered him; it was the mention of who came to their aid.

"Eric Porter is still in town?"

"He never left," she replied.

They'd never been friends but he knew Eric had liked his wife. He'd gone out of his way to speak to her even though she was married. He mostly did it when Sam was away on tour. It was creepy. He'd discovered this through a friend who had seen them together on numerous occasions down at a local café. Here was Richard accusing him of cheating but Sam could have quite easily made accusations against Helen except he didn't — he knew where Helen's loyalty was and the fact that she hadn't got hitched in all the time they'd been apart was proof of that. Sam knew she still loved him but that wasn't enough. Blood was thicker than water and her naivety to think her father wouldn't lie was what had caused her to believe his video — putting the final nail in the coffin on their marriage.

"By the way, did you see the power come back on?" Anna asked

"It came on?"

"Not for long, but yeah," she said.

It was a small glimmer of hope but it was something. Perhaps the government was finally getting on top of the issue. Maybe soon the lights would come on and this would all be nothing but a bad dream. And maybe they wouldn't have to fight for their lives.

Chapter 5

Twenty-seven years he'd served. Howard Boone felt like a prisoner in his own town. *What we are doing is for your safety and protection,* Mayor Underwood had said.

What a bunch of horseshit.

Had it just been the curfew he might not have had any issue, but with rumors swirling that all firearms would be collected in the city to avoid opposition, he aimed to send a clear message to Underwood.

"That's not going to happen, not without a fight," he mumbled under his breath.

Geared up in camouflage fatigues, he blended seamlessly into his surroundings. A hard afternoon sun beat down causing beads of sweat to form on his brow as he waited for his brothers Keith and Carl Boone.

He glanced at his watch for the third time. They were meant to be there forty minutes ago. *Where the hell are you?* he thought. He'd positioned himself in the tree line of the woods just beyond Richard's home. He'd told them to meet him at just after one. Howard lay on his side thinking of all the shady jobs he'd done for Richard, and the trouble he had caused in the city over the years. From Richard's pro-immigrant stance to clamping down on landlords, he had screwed up the town. Was it any wonder why his successor upped and left at the first sign of trouble? At least with the former mayor, Michael Lansbury, he'd listened. He was easy to sway, and had he not skipped town, perhaps there might have been hope.

Underwood just acted like a law unto himself.

Why they had allowed him to step back into the role of mayor was beyond him.

Well it ended today. He wasn't going to sit by and watch him dictate.

Howard lit another cigarette and scanned the trees for his brothers.

He eyed the rear of Underwood's mammoth home with jealousy. Underwood was so full of himself — living in a seven-bedroom home, in one of the most coveted neighborhoods in town, driving classic cars and flaunting his wealth in front of them. It was disgusting. But that wasn't all. Oh no, he knew the game Underwood had been playing, cheating on his wife. He knew the truth about him. He presented himself as a family man full of values in order to get elected but behind the scenes he was having sex with a long line of women, one of which was Elizabeth Myers, a woman that he'd been close with, a woman he could see himself settling down with. Sure, Elizabeth was in the wrong business and he'd told her countless times to get out of it, but still, to learn that Underwood had been seeing her only incited his hate for the man even more.

Boone heard a rustle behind him; he grabbed his pistol in time to see his numbskull brothers running at a crouch towards him. "Where the hell have you two been?"

"We ran into some trouble," Keith said.

"Like?"

Keith looked over his shoulder. "It doesn't matter."

Howard looked at Carl. "You better not be using

again. I need you to be clearheaded."

"I haven't touched the stuff. I swear, Howard."

He nodded, narrowing his eyes; he didn't trust either of them. Carl had wound up with a nasty drug habit a few years back after losing his kid in a car accident. At first Howard didn't ride him over it. He understood the pain of loss but when it started to affect his work and jeopardize some of his side businesses — namely rental properties — he came down on him hard.

As for Keith, he helped him at the butcher shop and assisted Carl in maintaining the apartments. At one time they had more than eleven until Underwood stepped in and started enforcing a law on what landlords could or couldn't do. It had eaten into his profits and forced several of his apartments to be closed down until they met certain building and city codes.

"Come on, let's go. Richard left about an hour ago. Who knows when he'll be back? We need to do this quick. Did you bring what I asked?" Howard asked.

Keith lifted up a plastic bag and the cans inside rattled.

They dashed across the rear yard. Carl went around the front to make sure the coast was clear before Howard smashed the window on the rear door and entered. As soon as he was inside he took out a can of paint spray and went into the largest room in the house — the living room — and sprayed on the wall a portion of the Second Amendment. When he was done he stepped back and smiled.

He tapped his brother Keith on the shoulder. "You think he'll get the message?"

Keith laughed and over the course of the next twenty minutes they went on a rampage smashing, tearing and tossing furniture out the back. But that was just them warming up. He stepped inside the garage and looked at three classic cars. Oh this was going to be good. He reared back a baseball bat and went to work on the cars.

When he was done, Howard looked upon the engine parts, crumpled metal, shattered glass and ripped-up seats and wiped sweat from his brow.

Keith stepped in. "The portable generator? Should

we…"

"Don't destroy it. I want it."

"But Howard, that's going to weigh a ton carrying that back through the woods," Carl moaned.

"That's why I brought you two."

This wasn't the first time he'd had a disagreement with Richard.

As Howard took a sledgehammer he found in the basement and plowed it through a door he thought back to the last night Richard had paid him to do his dirty work. Back then they were on good terms. He'd take care of business and Richard would pay him well. Back then they thought they had an understanding; that was, until he ripped him off.

"I know you have ties in the sex trade, make some calls. I'll make all the rest of the arrangements. All you have to do is make it happen," Richard said.

"How much you paying?"

"I'll give you five thousand."

"Five thousand? Forget it. I'm not going out on a limb for

five thousand. People talk in this town. If this gets linked back to me, my business will be over."

"Don't you think I've thought of all that? You'll be fine. I already have an alibi."

Richard had arranged to meet him at a truck stop just north of Breckenridge. It was a greasy spoon diner that rarely saw anyone from the local area besides truckers and lot lizards doing their rounds. Richard stood out in his expensive suit and overpriced cologne.

Howard shook his head. "Twenty grand, and I want ten at the start and ten when it's done."

"Twenty grand? Are you out of your mind?"

"Hey, you're lucky I don't go to the city council and tell them about this."

Richard stared back at him. "You know, Howard, I could make things real difficult for you. I would recommend you tread carefully."

"Twenty grand or find someone else. Though I doubt you know anyone with my connections."

Howard knew he had him. The fact was the only reason

Richard knew Howard had connections in the sex trade was because he was screwing Elizabeth. At some point his name was dropped, and that sleaze tried to capitalize on it.

"Why him?" Howard asked.

"That doesn't matter."

"Just curious."

"Well keep your curiosity to yourself."

"It's just that I imagine your daughter isn't going to like it. What did he do to you?"

Richard stared back at him and without missing a beat said, "Married my daughter."

Howard burst out laughing and rocked back in his seat. He leaned forward and took a scoop of his apple pie and shoveled it away. "Underwood, you are one screwed up individual. Why don't you tell her to leave him? Pay him off. Or better still just ignore him."

"It's not as easy as that."

Howard shook his spoon at him. "I rarely see him around. Seems like that's a good thing."

"That's the problem."

They stared at each other and Howard broke into laughter. "You really are one twisted fuck. So, do we have a deal?"

"Twenty grand. I'll drop off ten this week. But I want the video, you hear me? And if word gets out that I was behind it, I will burn you to the ground, do you understand?"

"Burn me to the ground. Yeah, I get it. Though I would like to see you do it."

Richard leaned across the table. "You're not the first and you won't be the last. Just do the job, keep your mouth closed and you'll be twenty grand better for it."

He snorted as Richard looked down at the plate of food the waitress had given him. He pushed it away without taking a bite.

"You know, Richard, I figure that someone who is willing to pay twenty grand might be worth more."

It was in that moment that he understood the real power behind Richard, and the reason why even after all these years he hadn't crossed him. Without saying a word he gave a nod to something or someone over Howard's shoulder and the bell above the café door let out a shrill. In walked a huge barrel-shaped individual in a leather jacket, with tattoos up the side of his neck. He sat down beside Howard, making him look small.

Richard leaned in. "I really hoped we didn't have to go here but I figured you might pull something like that. Asking for twenty grand is a joke but I let that slide because I know you can get the job done, however, let me be very clear here. I don't like you. I don't trust you. We are not friends and once this is over we will not speak again about this event and if you do, not only will I burn your businesses to the ground but also you and my friend here will get acquainted. Do I make myself clear?"

Howard swallowed and cast a sideways glance. The guy looked as if he'd walked straight out of the prison yard.

"I'm cool with that."

With that said Richard tossed down a few dollars on the table to cover their meals and left the café. And true to his word he showed up later that week with ten grand and green lit him for the night Sam would be at the bar.

Richard had arranged to have a meal with Sam, and a couple of drinks.

Elizabeth, desperate for cash and eager to earn herself a week's worth of blow, had agreed to show up despite being an old friend of Sam's. Howard remembered it like it was yesterday.

He stood outside the bar with Elizabeth and gave her the drug for his drink.

"Slip this into his drink, keep him happy, and leave the rest to me."

"You know, Howard, I don't like this."

"Then I'll have one of your pals do it. I'm sure they could use the money."

He pulled out a bag of coke and hung it in the air like a carrot on the end of a stick. "I'm guessing you won't want this either."

Elizabeth snatched it out of his hand.

"That's a good girl." Howard looked through the window of the bar and restaurant. "Look, I know you like him but believe me when this is all over you will understand why it

had to be done. Now go on in there, sway that ass of yours and make polite conversation. For old times' sake."

Richard left the bar, and glanced at Howard on the way out.

Howard gave him the thumbs-up before he slipped into his car and drove away.

From beyond the window he watched as Elizabeth entered with a group of friends and made eye contact with Sam. Plied with alcohol and pleased to see an old school friend, he was like putty in her hands. He had no idea what line of work she was in or the crazy coke habit she had. All he saw was an old friend wanting to have a drink.

It didn't take long, less than ten minutes before she managed to drop the GHB into his drink. Seeing him unravel and give way to the drug coursing through his body was the best part. Her pals had been paid to carry him out of the bar to a waiting vehicle, which would take Sam and Elizabeth to a fifty dollar a night, bug-infested motel on the outskirts of Breckenridge. Clothes were removed, photos were taken and a video was put together.

In some ways Howard felt sorry for the guy. He didn't care about his marriage but he understood what it was like to be manipulated by Richard Underwood. The guy was a leech on the skin of society, sucking it dry and serving no purpose.

That night Sam's marriage was ruined. No man could have explained that video, or the photos of him chatting to Elizabeth in the bar.

And true to his word, Richard gave him the rest of his money.

But that wasn't where it ended.

Howard should have known that Richard wouldn't take the risk of having him drop his name as being the one behind it. It wasn't long before his apartments were being shut down for code violations and a health inspector showed up at his store and slapped him with a hefty fine.

He knew Richard was behind it, trying to move him along, run him out of town but that wasn't happening. Just like he wasn't going to create new rules that would require the folks of Breckenridge to hand over their firearms. Sure it was just a rumor swirling around but he knew how Richard operated. It always started as a rumor.

"Howard. Howard!" Keith shouted, snapping him back into the present moment.

"What?"

"It's done. Let's go before someone shows up."

He looked around at the devastation. Huge holes in the walls, spray paint covering every surface, carpets torn up, furniture rolled out into the backyard, windows smashed and Carl had even taken a piss in his kitchen.

As Howard backed out of there and melted into the tree line, returning to his vehicle on Ski Hill Road, he felt a great deal of satisfaction.

This was just the beginning.

Chapter 6

Juliet – 01 Launch Control Center

Nine miles west of Peetz, Colorado, seventy-five feet below ground in a nuclear bombproof bunker the size of a shipping container, Missileer 1st Lieutenant Mia Hart sat before a communication system console nervously anticipating the warning order. Since the power had gone out across the country they'd been on high alert. She and one other member of the launch control crew had been living off a limited amount of food from topside. The emergency food below the floor was rarely used unless somehow they became locked behind two blast-proof doors.

The sound of an air-conditioning unit pumping cold air through the capsule dominated. Before the grid went down the whole system drew power from an outside source. They'd been running the diesel backup generator for the last ten days, and had only had one shift change since the event. Why? She'd still like to know that. They'd had little communication with higher-ups and something told them they wouldn't know any more until the lights came back on. Working on rotating twenty-four hour shifts, three days a week inside that submarine style container, was hard enough on an ordinary day but that had only got worse with the attack on the country.

It didn't help that all the equipment was dated, and many things were broken, like a few of the communication systems, and the tiny airplane sized toilet because there had been a recent leak and they hadn't got around to getting it repaired.

Mia breathed in the musty smell of military-grade paint and stagnant air.

This was Mia's first time being in the capsule.

"I swear once this is over I'm putting in a request to be posted somewhere else," Mia said.

"Ah, you worry too much. Besides, look at it this way, you only have three years of doing this before you can go to another missile base and move on to become an instructor, or an evaluator. And if you make it through that, well the world is your oyster. Hell, you might even work with the test squadron in California or one of the NATO forces in Europe," Lieutenant Douglas said. He was laying back on the single mattress trying to get some shuteye. There always had to be one person at the ready just in case enemy missiles were launched. In such an event they would only have minutes to fire back. "In the nine years I have been doing this job we have never once had to launch. You'll soon get the hang of it."

"We're ten days into this and the power still isn't up."

"Came up this morning."

"Yeah for all of ten minutes."

"That's a good sign," Douglas said. "It means they're working on it. Look at it this way, Mia. If the Russians wanted to nuke us they would have done it by now. They've had plenty of opportunities. I'm telling you this isn't the Russians. Probably somewhere in some dank basement an IT guy is going to get his ass served to him on a platter for falling asleep on the job and hitting the wrong button. Happens all the time in my neighborhood. Do you know how many times the Internet and phone system goes down where I am?"

She shrugged, her eyes firmly fixed on the aged panels in front of her. Some were a light blue, and some were a pale military green. She'd imagined when she took the job that the system would be high end. It was 2018 for goodness' sakes. The world had advanced. The nuclear system hadn't.

"Four times. I kid you not. It goes down once a week."

"Your phone line?"

"Our phone is connected with our Internet so if that goes down, so does the landline."

"You need a separate line."

"That would have cost more."

Mia chuckled. "What, twenty bucks?"

"Twenty is what they advertise. You got to look at the fine print, Mia. That's where they get you. Oh, I'm sorry, sir. We forgot to tell you that there is a fee for connection, and a fee for buying us a keg on the weekend," he said in a mocking tone. "You name it. They are notorious for their fees."

"Change company."

"It's not that easy."

"Of course it is," Mia said. She quickly changed the subject. "Douglas, doesn't it freak you out that we have in our pockets computers the size of our hand with ten thousand times the computing power than these rusted industrial stacks in front of us?"

"Nope. Were you sleeping when they trained you? That computer in front of you not only handles the missiles but it is completely unhackable. No one knows the language of these machines, it isn't connected to the Internet, unlike your cell phone." He folded his arms behind his head and breathed in deeply. It was just another ordinary day on the job for him, and yet she was freaking out inside. Had the country's grid not been down she might have taken it in stride but something wasn't right about it and the powers that be weren't saying what was going on. Contrary to what some thought, not everyone in the military knew what the left hand was doing. All of them knew just enough to do the job before them. They knew the risks but that's what they signed up for; to serve and protect, and if push came to shove and she got that command she wouldn't hesitate to turn the key.

She glanced at the box and went through the routine in her head of what they would do if they got the order. It would come through on paper on one of the ancient teletypewriters; she would then have to unlock a red box that contained the launch codes and two sets of keys. It had to match the incoming encrypted message otherwise they didn't move ahead. If all were good, both of them would have to enter the launch code simultaneously on a panel in front of her and then get on a conference call with another squadron to make sure they had a valid launch order. If they got the go-ahead, two keys would be inserted and turned in unison, and the other launch crew would do the same on their end to launch the ten ICBMs from that launch facility.

They were one of forty-five launch facilities spread out over 10,000 square miles of remote ranch land and wind farms. She was one of ninety missilers sitting on alert ready to launch at command. The isolated post was a good two hours away from the Air Force base, three miles from the nearest silo, and nine from the furthest.

"Yeah but we also know there are still a couple ways for people to get control of these ICBMs," Mia said.

"Oh please. No one is going to be stupid enough to go digging down for the HICS cabling. And if they do, it's pneumatically pressurized with air and monitored by us. We'll get an alert and security will head out."

"By then it could be too late."

He laughed. "We have motion detectors out there."

"Not for the cabling. It spans across 10,000 square miles of farmland."

Douglas cast a glance over at her for the first time in several hours.

Mia reached for the rotary phone. "Maybe I should

call up, and…"

Above ground was a six-man alert response team responsible for the security of the ten missiles and responding to any sensor alerts from Mia or Douglas.

"Put the phone down, Mia. They are already stressed out enough as it is. All they need is for you to fill their head with illogical ideas. No one is going to be stupid enough to do that. And it's debatable about whether or not it could be done."

"Debatable? Not according to the former head of STRATCOM. He said that our nuclear missiles could be hacked, launched and detonated without authorization. And he said that there were only two realities in today's world, either you've been hacked and won't admit it, or you're being hacked and you don't know yet."

Douglas swung his legs off the bed and got this serious look on his face. "When I was told I was getting someone new down here I didn't expect them to send someone who would question every goddamn thing. Enough, lieutenant."

"I wouldn't be questioning if the country's grid wasn't down and we had received a shift change in the past four days. There are thousands of lives on the line here."

"Don't you think I know that?"

She looked back at her console. "We have 450 missiles online. It doesn't take much to launch them. I'm just saying, taking these missiles offline and removing the warheads would help. It would only take a couple of hours to get them ready but at least that way no one could launch them by mistake and hackers couldn't gain access."

"Sounds good in theory except there is a major flaw in what you just said. What if Russia or one of the other countries decided to fire upon the USA? Huh? It would take only thirty minutes for an ICBM to arrive in the USA from Russia. Right now we can fire back within minutes. Besides, it's not like we can do anything about it. We are just the trigger team. That's it."

Mia shook her head. She had a five-year-old son at home with her husband. She loved her country and would do anything to protect it but even she was starting to have doubts about the situation they were in.

"But it wouldn't be the first time things went wrong. I'm just saying."

He scoffed. "That was back in 2010 and it wasn't a hack. It was a temporary interruption with our ability to monitor them. It wasn't a big deal."

"Losing contact with fifty Minuteman III's I would say is a big deal."

She recalled it hitting the news long after it had been rectified. No one knew if the enemy was trying to disable or launch the missiles. It threw Global Strike Command into a state of panic.

"Mia, this whole command system was designed back in the '60s and '70s. What do you expect? Things break down. Turns out it was just an improperly installed circuit card. And I might add if it wasn't for that, we wouldn't know about the vulnerabilities."

She caught him by his own words.

"So you admit there are vulnerabilities."

"I didn't say that."

"But you alluded to it."

He shook his head. "After this is over. I'm going to be having words with the higher-ups. I don't think you're fit for this job."

"What, because I'm a woman?"

"No. Because you're annoying," he said rolling back over and pulling the red blackout curtain across so he didn't have to converse with her. But she wasn't done. She turned in her seat and yanked it open.

"Surely you must be worried. It's been ten days."

He groaned. "Mia, seriously, give me a break. I want to get some sleep."

She got up and paced, keeping an eye on the console. She couldn't drop her guard for even a minute.

"All right. But just answer this one thing. Do you believe that the ICBMs are vulnerable because of the aging command-and-control technology?"

"I already told you, the computer system that we work with is unhackable."

"I understood that. What I'm speaking about is the missile silos' radio receivers and HICS cables."

He rolled over and looked at her and clenched his jaw.

"Yes, there is a potential that someone with the capability could breach the fire-walled system but they would need to have a strong reason and a determined team willing to die."

"So Liam Westborough was right."

He rolled his eyes. "Why did I know you were going to drop that name? Listen, the guys is a sleaze. He got fired from here and instead of doing the right thing and keeping his mouth shut, he put out a book and let his gums flap on multiple radio interviews. Take everything he says with a grain of salt."

"He worked here."

"I know. I worked alongside him."

"Then why would he lie?"

"Because he wants to sell books and get back at the Air Force for screwing up."

"He says it was nothing to do with him and it was a

missile technician who dropped a socket."

"And it plunged seventy feet and pierced the side of the missile, punctured and released pressurized rocket fuel. I already know that. But there is a lot about that incident that he didn't tell you about. Like the fact that he wasn't manning his station at the time; he'd stepped out and was chatting with the technician."

"He said he had to use one of the toilets upstairs because this one was broke."

"He had a job to do, and interfering and shooting the breeze with a tech was not part of it."

Mia nodded. "But that doesn't take away from what he said. The radio antenna at the unmanned missile silo is designed to identify targets, arm, and launch if there is a breakdown inside this capsule. He said that that it could allow hackers to prevent a loss of control over the missiles."

"Potentially."

"C'mon, sir, you and I both know that it's true."

He groaned and shook his head.

"And what about the thousands of cables underground connecting all the missile silos with the launch control centers?"

"It's six foot underground."

"And?"

"It has a limited amount of bandwidth. It might be old but it's secure."

"But if someone does manage to tap into one of the cables and gain access to the conduits, they could control, target, enable and fire the missiles."

"Yes but it won't happen."

"Famous last words," she said, turning back to the console. Her views on the military had changed a lot since she'd joined the Air Force. At one time she thought they were light years ahead. She'd imagined she would see technology that the public wasn't aware about, and be privy to information that only those in the higher-ups would hear about, but it was the complete opposite. She was nothing but a number — an important part of the overall machine but just another cog in the works. As her eyes glazed over all the old equipment she couldn't help wonder what changes they would make when it came time to update this all and bring it into the twenty-first century. She'd heard word that it was going to happen but what was said and what was eventually done were two different things. Promises were broken all the time as budgets were cut and finances were reassigned. She was sure that most of it was going to the fat cats in Washington, the ones who called the shots but never got blood on their hands.

Mia sighed, she felt like an executioner, ready to flip the switch.

She sank back into her seat and heard the curtain behind her slide across.

"Don't wake me up unless it's an emergency."

"Yeah, whatever."

Mia hadn't wanted to be a missiler. She and several of her classmates had wanted to go to medical school but her parents had other ideas. After joining the Air Force and getting her assignment she would have been lying to say she didn't regret signing up. It felt like a mismatch. She'd studied math and linguistics and had no idea about missiles. It wasn't glamorous or desired. It meant working eight shifts a month, getting no weekends, and there were no holidays. It was only after she got assigned did a few of her colleagues tell her it was considered a dead-end job.

No sooner had she looked away from her console than a red light started flashing off to her left. An alarm rang out, and Douglas nearly fell out of his bed. She knew instantly what that meant — the motion sensors had gone off. Someone or something was on the property.

Chapter 7

He was furious and he knew who was behind it.

Richard saw the smashed windows long before he stepped inside with Eric in his shadow. An hour earlier he'd been overseeing the work at the shelter when he got word from a neighbor.

"I know it was him."

"You don't know that for sure," Eric said. "There were a lot of people at the town hall meeting who were against you."

Richard wouldn't listen to reason. He stopped to pick up a framed photo of him and his wife. The glass was cracked, and the frame broken. He removed the photo and tossed the rest, then moved into the living room where he looked at the message sprayed on the wall. Then it dawned on him. Richard hurried down the hallway and burst into his garage. His stomach dropped. *No. No!*

He shook his head, feeling his blood boil inside. Heads

were going to roll for this. After all he had done for them. He wasn't ready to point the finger but he was damn sure Sam was behind it.

"Bullshit. We went an entire week without any issues. And then Sam shows up, we get into a little confrontation and he reacts. Well, he's stepped over the line this time."

Leaving Eric in the living room he went into his basement and approached the far side of the room. He glanced over his shoulder to make sure Eric wasn't there before he pushed in an ordinary stone on his fireplace. There was a click. Across the room a section of his library shelves popped out. He went over and opened it to reveal a large safe. A few turns and it clicked open. Inside were several legal envelopes, stacks of cash, and a Glock 22. He took it out and slammed a magazine into the chamber, closed the safe and headed back upstairs.

"Eric," he said, gesturing for him to follow. In the kitchen he began searching for a bottle of bourbon. He found it on the ground, smashed to pieces. It was over forty years old. *Bastards,* he thought as he crouched and looked inside an empty cupboard for more of his stash.

"What is it?"

"On the table. Take it."

Richard got up and looked at him. Eric frowned as he gazed at the Glock 22.

"What's that for?"

"You remember what I said the night we buried the kid?"

He shook his head so Richard went over to him and placed a hand on his shoulder. "I said that one day there might come a time when I need you to do something for me."

He clued in immediately and quickly backed up from the gun, raising his hands.

"No. No. I'm not killing anyone for you. I'm not stepping over that line."

"Eric. Look around you. The line has already been crossed. An attack on me is an attack on you and everyone else that I work with. Now I want you to do something for me."

"I'm sorry, I can't be a part of it."

Richard's brow pinched together and he leaned against the breakfast counter. "You act as if you have a choice. Remember, you came to me after you killed that kid. I could have turned you in but I didn't. The only reason you are not behind bars right now is because of me." He straightened and walked over to Eric and cupped a hand around his neck pulling his head tight against his own. "We have to stick together. This is just the beginning. I was speaking with the chief today about the situation in the town. It's got worse, Eric. Much worse. Home invasions. Rape. Beatings. It won't be long before someone is killed. That could be you."

He let those words linger. He knew how to leverage his fears against him. He'd seen it in Eric's eyes. Although Eric knew the law like the back of his hand — not even he could wiggle his way out of the situation he'd got himself in.

Richard continued. "The jail cells are already starting to fill up. Under the circumstances it wouldn't be surprising if a mob wanted your head for what you did to that kid."

"It was an accident."

"I know it was. And so will this be," he said taking the gun and placing it into his hand. "Tonight, I want you to kill him. No mistakes."

He kept shaking his head like he was in shock.

"But…"

"I'll arrange it all. We have a meeting tonight to discuss the situation. I want you there. Maybe I can draw him away to get an answer if he's decided to help the chief or not. When everyone is inside, you'll take the shot. I'll say I didn't recognize the shooter."

"That's ridiculous."

"Unless you have a better idea."

"But."

"No buts, Eric. I want it done and you're going to do it. Or, I can go and speak with Chief Sanchez and let him know where the body is buried and that you came to me to confess. That would be a real shame. I don't want to do that."

"Richard, c'mon. Don't you think this is a bit extreme? Okay, so your house got messed up. You can bounce back from that. No one has been hurt. Think about what you're asking me to do."

He smiled. "You think I want to do this?"

"Then don't. Report him to Sanchez. Toss him in jail."

"How do I prove it? Huh? Anyone could have done this, Eric."

"Exactly!" he yelled at the top of his voice. "And yet you are acting as if you know it's him just because he's taken your granddaughter away."

"It's not just that."

"No? What is it then, huh? Because I'm starting to think Helen was right about you."

Richard's eyes narrowed. "Is that so?"

"Yeah."

He rolled his bottom lip and took a step back and looked around. "All right then, come out with it. What did she say?"

"She said you were controlling her life. She said you blamed Sam for your wife's death."

"He played a role."

"She died from cancer, Richard. For God's sake, man!"

There was a long stretch of silence between them.

"So are you going to do it or not?" Richard asked avoiding the discussion any further. He was done talking.

"Richard. Please."

"Yes or no?"

Eric tried to turn it around on him. "Your DNA is all over that kid as well."

He smiled. "Oh that's how you're going to play this?"

"Well look at what you're asking me to do!" Eric bellowed back.

"And remember what you asked me to do. I helped you."

"It was different. I didn't ask you to take a life."

"No, you just wanted me to cover it up. Make it go away. Well now I'm asking you to make something go away. But…" he turned and walked over the window, a smile forming on his face. "If you would rather not, fine. I'm sure we can see what Sanchez will say." He didn't have to wait there long. Eric was weak. Weak people always buckled. It was in their nature. Not him. Over the years he'd grown thick skin, weathered the storms of change and faced all manner of trials. This was a walk in the park.

"I'll do it but after this, we are done."

"Good lad," he said turning around. "Let's not discuss tomorrow. Let's talk about how we'll do this." He drew him in and began to lay out how it would go down.

Was it extreme? Maybe. But in his mind, Sam was like a disease that wouldn't go away. Since he'd returned he'd already placed his granddaughter's life in jeopardy. He wasn't going to let him take her away from him. She was all he had left, and he would fight to hold on to that.

* * *

It took him over an hour to get loose from his binds. Blake rose to his feet from the smashed chair and dropped the piece of glass that he'd used to cut through the ropes around his arms and feet. He hurried across to his son who was slumped over and tore through the ropes, slicing his own hands in the process. Aidan's body sank into his arms, a limp mass of bloodied flesh. His clothes were soaked and partially dry. Tears flowed as he held on to his kid and cried out. Thorn had taken everything from him. His wife, his kid, and now his freedom — it would only be a matter of hours before the military would swarm his home and steal him away.

But that wasn't what he feared the most.

It was the repercussions of his actions on American lives.

He hadn't just killed his wife and son; he'd hit the switch on the countdown to the demise of America. As soon as those missiles launched, Russia would retaliate and there wouldn't be a goddamn thing America could do about it. With no power, no communication and nothing to protect them, it would start an all-out war. The UK, and other countries that were considered the USA's ally, would come to their aid and all hell would break loose.

Blake remained there holding his son and weeping.

He didn't care whether he lived or died now; all that mattered to him was stopping Thorn.

* * *

It wasn't the first time the motion sensors had gone off. Senior Airman Matthews and Airman First Class Brunson grabbed their gear and headed out to the Peacekeeper armored vehicle. They were used to doing security sweeps. More often than not it was just tumbleweed, a bird, or an animal grazing that set off the motion detectors so they usually weren't concerned, however, that evening both were expecting the worst. While they went out, the third member of their team would remain at the Launch Control Support Building checking the cameras and providing additional support to the launch crew. The other three weren't on shift and were in their rooms when the alarm went off. Like all of the security response teams, they were wearing camo fatigues, had backpacks, and were carrying M4 rifles and

M9 pistols.

There was a lot of flat space to cover and it wasn't always easy to pinpoint an exact location so they had to keep their eyes peeled. With the sun going down visibility was low so they'd brought along necessary equipment to see.

Matthews was driving while Brunson gave directions.

"Take a left up here."

"I swear if this is another jackrabbit, I'm shooting it and putting it in a stew."

Brunson chuckled.

They drove for several miles until Brunson told him it was up ahead.

Matthews pulled off to the side of the road, hopped out and took out his NVG binoculars to scan the area from a distance, searching for any suspicious activity. Brunson got out and went over to the gate that led into vast farmland. He unlocked the chain and pushed it open before sprinting up the access road while Matthews provided cover from the Humvee. Matthews watched as

Brunson approached the exterior of the missile site and performed a routine check making sure it was secure before signaling for Matthews to advance.

Matthews jumped back in and drove on in scanning his field of vision.

He brought the Humvee up and kept it running while Brunson entered the fenced-in missile site and checked the topside looking for anything out of the ordinary. After he was finished conducting his sweep, Matthews would have to perform the same check to make sure he hadn't missed anything.

"All secure," Brunson said returning to the vehicle.

Matthews followed through doing one last check before they would head back. He got on the radio to communicate with Senior Airman Rigby.

"How we doing, Rigby? You see anything?"

"Nothing."

"Have you been through the history yet?"

There were multiple security cameras that allowed them to keep track of the silos for that facility. In the event of trouble Rigby would have contacted the base and called in heavily armed reinforcements who would arrive by helicopter in minutes.

"Checking now."

As Matthews made his way back, he was just about to give the thumbs-up when a vehicle came up behind the Humvee in the distance. Both of the airmen squinted and Matthews brought up his binoculars.

"Rigby, you seeing this?"

"Copy that."

"Stand by," Matthews said getting back into the vehicle and turning it around to block the entrance. They let it idle and positioned it sideways to prevent any access, and then Matthews got out. "Cover me."

Raising his M4, he brought his finger to the trigger and kept it ready to engage.

He cupped a hand over his eyes. The glare from the final rays of the sunset made it hard to see the occupants but he could make out through the NVG binoculars that the van had the word Boeing on the side of it. He knew that they along with Northrop had got the contract to replace the ICBMs and they'd been informed they'd see them but not at this time of the day. What the hell were they doing out here?

As they got closer he put up a hand to indicate for them to stop. They slowed their vehicle and looked back at Brunson, and gave him a nod for him to join him. Cautiously they approached the vehicle with their rifles raised. The window dropped on the driver's side and a guy in blue engineer's clothing waved to them.

"Driver, turn off the engine," Matthews said.

The engine died.

Brunson went to the passenger side while Matthews approached the driver's side. Brunson walked around the back and then returned to the passenger side.

"Sorry guys, we were meant to be out here earlier today but got held up at another job."

"We don't have any information on a crew coming out."

"Shit." He turned to his buddy in the passenger side.

Both of them looked like average, hard-working Americans. One had some oil on the side of his neck. Matthews scanned the inside. There was a pack of cigarettes on the dashboard and a newspaper on the seat between them. "I knew they would screw it up. Truth is we were meant to be out here yesterday but the job at Malmstrom set us back a day. We were going to wait until tomorrow but why put off what you can get done today, right?"

"You got IDs?" Matthews asked.

"Yeah," he turned.

"Sir, keep your hands on the steering wheel."

"Martin, can you get it?"

"It's just in the glove compartment."

"Slowly," Matthews said. He got back on his radio. "Rigby, you got anything about Boeing doing any work on the missiles?"

"Nope," he replied.

They brought out IDs and handed them over and Matthews flashed a light over them. He'd seen a couple before as some of them had come out and been introduced to the crew so they would be familiar with those who'd be doing work.

"Why's Boeing working on the missiles in a power outage?"

"Got to protect our investment. It's our heads on the line."

"That's commitment," Matthews said handing over the IDs. "Last thing, what have you got in the back?"

"Just equipment, tools."

"Step out and open up."

"All right but there isn't much to show you."

They came around the back and he unlocked the doors. The windows were tinted so he couldn't see in. Matthews placed his finger on the trigger and backed up ready for the unexpected. The guy pulled back the doors and sure enough there was nothing inside except for racks of tools, wire and several cardboard boxes. "Told you."

"All right. Close it up. I'm afraid, though, I can't let you in."

"Oh come on, man. We just came all the way out here."

"Without authorization no one gets in."

"Would it help to speak to our boss?"

Matthews looked over at Brunson and he shook his head.

The guy continued rattling on about how it was going to set them back even more days and they really couldn't afford to…

"Matthews!" Rigby's voice bellowed over the radio disrupting his train of thought. "It's a setup."

He put a finger up to his ear. "Rigby, repeat."

Unknown to them but visible to Rigby, who had eyes on them, were two men emerging from underneath the van. Brunson's back was turned. He didn't stand a chance.

A sudden eruption of gunfire and he dropped.

Before Matthews could react a second flurry of bullets were unleashed taking him down. He coughed and spluttered, blood spilling out the corner of his mouth. He struggled on the ground, reaching for his rifle, when a heavy boot pinned it to the dusty ground. He twisted in time to see the barrel of a gun.

Crack!

Then darkness.

Chapter 8

The neighbors have better stuff? A frown appeared on Sam's forehead as he read the latest homemade sign that Chase had tapped into the ground near the front of the driveway.

"A deterrent is better than no deterrent, right?" he replied.

"Where is the deterrent in that, Chase?"

He stared back at it. "Well, it lets them know that…" He trailed off realizing how absurd it was. It was the kind of thing that might be bought from a gag store.

Both laughed and Sam patted him on the back. "You have a long way to go, grasshopper. C'mon, give me a hand," he said before walking down the driveway.

Over the past few hours he'd been attaching window bars to the front of the home, a job that Anna was meant to do but she'd got sidetracked with helping out at the emergency shelter. While other residents in Breckenridge in the first ten days were focusing on the basics like food and water, Sam had set about seeking out companies in the town that offered hardware that could be used to secure the home. Over the past few days they'd already been out to gather items that would be useful for fortifying the property like barbed wire for the top of fencing, reinforced locks for the windows, striker plates for the front and rear doors, and cameras that would operate off the generator.

As Sam screwed in the last bar, he stepped back and admired their handiwork.

The property was beginning to look like Fort Knox but that was the whole point. He didn't want to stay up at night, and work a rotating shift just to protect themselves from intruders, and he didn't want to come home to find the place stripped bare.

Sam's mind circled back to the chief.

He'd given a lot of thought to the request; he knew that it wasn't a large department. They couldn't have had more than twenty-five sworn officers and those that were on shift at any given time would fluctuate based on vacation, court duties and days of the week. They only worked four, ten-hour shifts a week but with the situation, the entire department would be working overtime.

He'd seen the way Anna had stepped up to the plate to help. Helen had definitely instilled good traits in her. For someone who had been living away from home for many years, she didn't act self-entitled like what he might have expected from someone who came from a wealthy family. She was grounded, grateful for what she had and thoughtful just like her mother. He hadn't got around to speaking to her about Helen's death. In the days after discovering she'd passed away, he'd heard Anna at night crying but when morning came and he tried to speak to her she would brush it off and change the subject. She was doing what he was good at, hiding how he really felt. It was easier that way. At least it had been in his line of work. He couldn't fall apart out in the field. He had men that relied on him, families that expected to see their husbands come home. Sam had learned earlier in his career to push down his emotions and control them. Emotional reactions led to mistakes and mistakes got people killed.

Mason slapped him on the back. "Not bad. Not bad at all. I certainly will sleep better tonight. Which reminds me, are we going to the town hall meeting?"

Sam nodded. "Yeah, I want to find out what's happening."

"You know he'll be there."

"Of course."

"And that doesn't bother you?"

He gave a broad smile. "Mason, he might be at the helm of this town but he isn't in control. That's all an illusion." Sam turned and looked off into the horizon. The sun had all but set leaving only a few bands of light filtering through black smoke that billowed high and drifted over pines. "Take a look for yourself. The wheels are already in motion. I'm interested to know how they plan to respond to it."

"I think it's obvious. They want folks like you and me out there risking our necks. You given much thought to what he asked?"

"Yeah," Sam replied. "I want to speak with Chief Sanchez directly, not when Richard is around. The guy is like a leech."

"Speaking of the leech. Heads up, we got company."

Sam turned to see Eric Porter with his arm wrapped around Richard who was holding a hand up to his head; his fingers were gloved in blood. Sam made his way over. And got a closer look at his head. There was a large gash, and his lip was busted up. "What happened?" Sam asked.

Eric was first to respond, "A home invasion. They beat him pretty bad and tore up his place. I arrived minutes after and managed to scare them off. I found him in the kitchen."

Richard latched hold of Sam, smearing blood on his jacket. "They're still out there. They headed north through the woods."

"Have you contacted the police?" he asked.

"No."

Sam turned to Mason. "Take him inside, I'm going to head over to the department and…"

"No," Richard said in a very stern tone.

"Are you serious?"

"They'll be gone by the time you get back."

Eric nodded. "He's right."

"How many were there?"

"Two guys, at least that's what I saw. There could be more."

Sam headed over to the house. "I'll get my rifle and we'll head out."

He hadn't made it within ten feet of the door when Anna came bursting out. "Grandfather!" She hurried over and gave Eric a hand bringing him inside.

"I should go with you," Eric said. "Show you where they went."

"All right. You know how to fire a weapon?" Sam asked.

Eric nodded.

"Mason, you think you can hold down the fort here?"

His brow pinched. "You want me to stay?"

"I'm going with you," Anna said. "Amanda, can you take care of him?"

"It's too dangerous," Eric added quickly. For once Sam was pleased that someone else said it and not him. Anna had come a long way in a short time and he was confident that she could handle herself but the thought of her getting hurt would have been too much. Besides, he was keen to have a conversation with Eric and find out what the situation was like between him and Helen prior to her death. It had been many years since he'd seen him. He didn't look the same. Years ago he was tall, and wiry but now he'd filled out, the result of good living. There were a few crow's feet at the corners of his eyes, and some strands of silver at his temples but that was about it.

Back when they were married he'd often heard that Eric was hanging around Helen, helping her out. He'd asked a neighbor of his to keep an eye on him and because nothing had ever given him cause for concern he didn't read much into it. Besides, it gave him some peace of mind to know that Helen had someone she could rely on. It was only when he heard that Richard was responsible for Eric seeing Helen that the pieces started to fall together. From that day forward he put his foot down.

The last conversation he'd had with Eric was after returning from an operation in Saudi Arabia. He'd waited until Eric was done working and approached him outside the lawyer's office. Although he remained composed, he made it clear in no uncertain words that he didn't want him hanging around Helen while he was away. At first Eric was caught off guard, nervous even. Then he became all defensive.

"What are you accusing me of?"

"I'm not accusing you of anything. I'm just telling you. It stops today."

"Look, Sam, I'm not stepping on your toes. Helen and I are just friends."

"Oh I'm well aware that Richard has a way of making arrangements. I'm just letting you know that when I'm not

around, I still know what's going on, if you get my drift."

"Fine. But I think Helen should be the one to decide."

"Helen is well aware of our conversation today. Just back off. Okay?"

"Is that a threat?"

"It's whatever you want it to be."

With that said, Sam turned and walked off into the crowd

Now, as he came out of the house with a rifle slung over his shoulder, he glanced at Eric and saw a different man. There was an air of confidence to him that could have only come from not having Sam around, and the approval and support of Richard.

Sam gave a wave to Mason and then hopped into the derby car.

He fired up the engine and was about to pull away when Anna slipped into the back. Sam twisted in his seat.

"Anna, what the hell are you doing?"

"I'm going with you."

"Like hell you are. Get out."

"You might as well drive on as I'm not getting out until we're at the house."

Eric looked back. "Your father has a point."

She shrugged. Sam knew there was no point fighting it. "You can stay at the house while we're in the field."

"Not happening."

He slammed the gearstick in drive and tore out of there. Richard's home was within walking distance but they wanted to get over there fast. If whoever had been behind the beating was out in the forest, they wouldn't get far. The terrain around the properties was rocky, and steep in areas.

"Were they armed?"

"Carrying rifles," Eric said.

"With the sun going down, there's a good chance they'll be using flashlights. Shouldn't be difficult finding them." He looked in his rearview mirror as they pulled into Richard's driveway.

Anna leaned forward between the two front seats, her eyes widening. "Holy shit."

The headlights on the car washed over the building and they took in the sight. It was a complete mess. Shattered glass scattered all over the driveway, furniture rolled out.

The first thing Sam did before heading into the woodland behind the house was to secure the house and make sure they hadn't returned to finish whatever they'd set out to do. It didn't take long. Flashlight beams bounced off the doors and walls as they made their way to the rear. It was even worse in the yard. The large concrete water fountain had been upended and was on its side and half of the living room furniture was outside. "They really went to town on this place. Did you see if they took anything?"

"I think I spooked them. I was packing," Eric said removing a Glock 22 from a holster around his waist.

"Okay, which way?" Sam asked.

Eric pointed and led the way. Anna followed; she was in the middle while Sam hung back at the rear to watch their backs. It was very possible they were still out there biding their time and waiting for another opportunity to return. He'd noticed that the two neighbors' homes were still intact which meant someone had targeted Richard. He'd seen the message sprayed on the wall.

"Whoever did it must think he's planning on taking people's weapons or preventing the community from carrying. What's the deal with that?" Sam asked.

Eric trudged through the gloomy dark forest pushing branches out of the way. The sound of the stream bubbling nearby could be heard.

"At the last town hall meeting, there were a number of people that objected to the curfew. With the increase in crime, Richard's in talks with Chief Sanchez to invoke some kind of law whereby residents will have to give up their weapons."

"Best of luck with that," Sam said. "Americans won't give up their guns, and they certainly aren't going to listen to some pompous asshole."

"Dad," Anna said.

"Sorry, Anna but it's true. The man is a nuisance to

society."

Eric scoffed. "He can be a pain in the ass but he gets things done in the city. He's a man of his word. That's for sure."

The smell of pine lingered in the air, and a cool breeze made the branches sway under a dark sky. Sam scanned the hilly, densely forested landscape. They continued walking for several miles, crossing over the creek before it became clear that they weren't going to find them.

"They could be anywhere," Anna said. "We should probably go back."

"No," Eric said. "Not before I check Valley Brook Cemetery."

"Why there?"

"I was speaking with an officer earlier today about the fires that had been lit across town. Apparently a group of teens on bikes were responsible. He managed to give chase but he lost them over on Breckenridge Terrace. A couple of the neighbors reported seeing them heading into the cemetery."

"The same ones I ran into?" Anna asked.

"Could be," Eric said."

"So did he check it out?"

"Who?" Eric asked.

"The cop," Sam said, noticing that Eric seemed a little nervous.

"Yeah, he did. They weren't there but that was earlier today."

"Then what makes you think they'll come back again?"

"After I dropped off Gene Landers I swung back around to the spot where he was attacked. I saw a kid on a dirt bike. He'd returned there."

"Did you approach him?" Anna asked.

"Hell no. I wanted to see what he was up to. I parked down the road. I think he must have dropped something because he was searching the ground. Anyway, he took off and I followed him."

"To the cemetery," Sam said.

He cast a glance over his shoulder. "Yep. I figure they must have some kind of hangout there."

"Odd place to congregate."

"Ah you know how these emo types are," he said. Sam stayed alert for trouble as they came out into a clearing and passed through a sparse area of trees before reentering heavy woodland again. "It's just beyond here," he said pointing forward.

Only the sound of their boots could be heard, and the occasional bird squawking in the trees.

"Were you there the day Helen died?" Sam asked.

Eric slowed his pace and glanced back, nodding.

"Were you seeing her?"

He scoffed. "Is that all that matters to you, Sam?"

"Just answer the question."

"No I wasn't. Richard had other ideas but Helen… she wasn't interested."

"Because she was dating someone else?"

"Wow, you really were out of the loop. No, Sam, Helen hadn't dated anyone since you left. Eleven years she had remained single. I…" He trailed off as if he was about to say something. When he spoke again they came over a rise and saw lights, and heard the sound of engines.

"Looks like we have them."

Chapter 9

The attack on the two airmen occurred simultaneously with Thorn's crew descending upon the launch control center. Unlike some of the military establishments in the 1960s and '70s era, the building didn't have bulletproof windows or reinforced walls; it was nothing more than drywall and glass, a building designed to house security. They stormed in, his men caught the other three airmen off guard, while Thorn entered the security control center, gun drawn and aimed at the remaining alert response member.

"I would advise you to put that radio down," Thorn said.

The security manager lowered it nice and slowly.

"That's it." Thorn grabbed it and tossed it to one of his men. Six of them had taken charge of the place while the others handled business. He could hear a commotion out in the hall as some of his team dragged out the remaining security members.

"Thorn," Dmitry called out. "All secure."

Thorn tapped Hector on the shoulder and pointed to Airman Rigby to make sure he kept an eye on him.

"What do you want done with them?" Dmitry called out.

"What do you think?"

As Thorn stepped back into the room, three rounds were fired and then silence dominated. The final member of the security team looked on in horror, his hands raised. "I…"

"Shut up. You're not going to die."

Thorn looked at the door with a small window, and pulled on the handle. It was locked. "Open the door."

"I can't do that," Rigby said.

Thorn brought the gun up to his face.

"Please. It's not that I wouldn't do it. I physically cannot open it. We give them codes when we arrive and they buzz us in if they match."

"What are the codes?"

The airman looked out into the night and swallowed hard.

"What are the CODES!" Thorn bellowed louder.

Rigby threw his hands up. "Okay. Let me get them." He shuffled forward in his chair to a drawer, unlocked it and pulled them out. "I'll have to phone through."

"While you're at it, let them know that the motion detectors were set off by an animal. All is well and the cook is bringing down the food early tonight."

The airman stared back at him as if he wasn't aware of how it operated. He knew enough to know that the two blast doors, seventy-five feet down below, only opened when a shift change occurred or food was brought in and they had a rule that one person couldn't be in the bunker alone, so they usually ate on the bridge area between the launch control center and the elevator, so they were in sight at all times.

Airman Rigby slid over to the phone and made the call.

"Lieutenant, this is Rigby." He looked up at Thorn

and Thorn shook his head noticing Rigby's hesitation. "The motion detectors were set off by an animal. All is well. I have the codes. The cook is coming down," he paused then yelled, "DON'T OPEN. It's a tr—" Before the word slipped his lips Hector fired a round and shot him.

Thorn stepped back, his eyes widening. "What have you done? You fucking idiot!"

"He was going to give away our…"

"He's the only way we get in!" Thorn grabbed him and threw him up against the door. It echoed. He tightened his grip around his throat; rage welling up inside of him. He hadn't spent this long going to these lengths to have it all screwed up now.

"Thorn, let him go!" Dmitry said entering the room and getting between them.

"I should kill him right now."

Hector gritted his teeth before Thorn released him. He took a few steps back and ran a hand over his head. "Oh my God," he said. He unleashed his anger by sweeping off several stacks of paperwork and folders to the ground and kicking a chair across the room.

"We don't need to get in," Hector said.

"You're an idiot. Did you not hear anything I said?" Thorn replied.

Hector frowned. "I heard you. We're going to tap into the HICS line. We can control it that way."

"Yeah but where are we going to go after the missiles launch? Huh?" Thorn said. "We will have less than thirty minutes to get away from here and find shelter before Russia reacts, by then it will be too late. The only way we survive this is by barricading ourselves in that bunker below ground until the dust settles. We needed to get in, Hector, and you just fucked it up!"

Hector looked back at him, a look of disbelief on his face.

Everything had gone to plan perfectly up until this point. The abduction of Blake Dawson, bringing down the interconnected infrastructure, nothing had gone wrong.

Thorn squeezed the bridge of his nose and perched on the edge of the table looking out into the night. His mind was swirling. He knew the crew below didn't have a means of calling for additional backup, it was all handled by security topside but that didn't mean they couldn't prevent them from moving ahead with their objective.

Thorn snatched up the phone and rang them.

A female picked up the phone. The blast doors only opened from the inside. "Open the blast doors now or the rest of them die," Thorn said.

He knew there were no cameras for the missile combat crew. The two lieutenants relied on the security manager. They only monitored and controlled the missiles.

There was a long pause. Thorn heard her talking with her co-worker, and when she came back on the line, her words weren't what he wanted to hear. "We can't do that."

"Then I guess you've just signed their death warrant."

He hung up. "Damn it!"

The other men looked at him, concerned expressions

spread throughout.

"What now?" Hector asked.

"Just give me time to think."

He exited the building to get some fresh air and have a cigarette. Thorn tapped one out and slid it between his lips and lit the end. The nicotine hit his system and he felt a wave of relaxation. Dmitry came out and joined him out by the Jeep.

"Are you going to change your mind?"

"Did I say that?" Thorn replied blowing smoke out the corner of his mouth. A hard wind blew across the flat plains, whipping his fatigues against his body and kicking up grit into his eyes.

"We can still do this. To hell with it," Dmitry said.

"Dmitry, you might have a death wish but I don't. There is no satisfaction if we're not alive to see the country break."

"It's already broken, my friend. If we leave the power grid down it's only a matter of time before Russia or an enemy of the US takes advantage of it. We've done our part."

"No we haven't. We have crippled them. They will bounce back from this. Give it enough time, they will clear the malware just like they did in the Ukraine. All we've done is disrupt. I want to destroy." He looked back at Dmitry. "Isn't that what you wanted for your country too?"

"Of course."

"Then we continue," Thorn said tossing his cigarette to the ground. A few golden sparks bounced as he made his way inside.

"What are you going to do?"

"Find the generator for this shit hole and turn it off. Then we'll see how long they can last in that capsule without air."

* * *

Sam shouldered his rifle and pressed on into the cemetery. Large tombstones marched away into the distance and concrete mausoleums blocked their view of the bikers. He could make out flashlights bouncing through the trees, and one of them had started a fire inside a steel drum.

"Are you sure they were armed?" Sam asked.

"Positive."

"They're just teens," Sam said squinting into the darkness. They certainly didn't look like a threat. They couldn't have been older than Anna.

Eric turned to Anna. "You saw what they did to Gene, tell him."

"They busted him up really bad," Anna said.

Eric said, "Gave him a concussion. The guy is in stable condition but he was lucky to survive."

They made it to a mausoleum and took cover so Sam could get a better look at what they were up against. Although he didn't imagine them causing any trouble, they were living in different times now. Not all cities and towns would resort to violence and theft as not everyone was the same. Doped-up individuals didn't think straight even when the law did exist, so would they act any different now?

"I'm going around," Eric said. "I'll cover you from the west."

"I'll take the east," Anna said.

"No you won't. It will put you in direct line of fire. Stay with me."

He approached from the south and told her to get behind him as he moved in on the group. There were four of them partying it up, drinking beer and acting like idiots. One was leaning against his bike, two were smoking weed and the other one was using a steel baseball bat and hacking away at a tombstone. Shadows danced on their faces as the fire licked up into the night sky.

"I'm telling you the cops haven't a clue," one of them said.

"I told you they wouldn't give us any trouble. They have their hands full as it is."

Out the corner of his eye, Sam could see Eric moving into position. He was packing a Glock 22 while Sam had an M4.

He didn't have to say anything to the guys. One of

them spotted him and alerted the others. Their heads whipped around and one of them put his hands up.

"Hey man, it's all cool."

It was an odd reaction for teens that were have supposed to have caused so much trouble. As he moved in he scanned them and noticed they weren't carrying rifles, or handguns. What the hell was Eric going on about?

"Get on the ground," Sam said.

"Look man."

One of them hopped up onto his bike and Sam unloaded a round in the air. The echo was enough to scare the living daylights out of him and his attempt at kick starting his bike stopped before it caught hold.

Sam hurried over keeping his handgun on him. "Get off the bike."

He slipped off putting his hands up.

"Which two was it?" Sam called out to Eric.

"I'm not sure. It was dark."

"Which of you two were involved in a home invasion on Iron Mask Drive?" he asked. All four of them shook their heads but said nothing.

"Come on now, otherwise you're all going in."

"We haven't gone anywhere near there," a guy with long blond dreadlocks said.

"You sure about that?"

"Positive."

"Are you a cop?" one of them asked.

"Nope."

The kid started chuckling. "Then why the fuck are you pointing a gun at us?"

"You carrying?" Sam asked.

"Nah man."

One of them looked like he was reaching for something.

Sam was about to caution him when a round went off, this time from Eric's weapon. A chunk of stone from a tombstone near them broke away and they all bounced back. "Whoa, whoa! Okay man, okay, we're cool."

Sam looked over to Eric who wasn't looking at the kids but at him. He lowered his weapon. Sam turned his head and glanced at the tombstone closest to him. "Something doesn't add up," Sam mumbled. "Eric, get over here."

"I'm fine here."

"Eric."

He moved out from behind the tombs and made his way over.

"Hey man, I know you. You're that lawyer in town."

"How very observant," he said glancing at Sam and Anna. "Look, I say we take them in. Hand them over to the cops."

Sam squinted. "You recognized they were bikers but can't recognize the two who ran away?"

Eric shook his head.

"Ah fuck this," one of them said jumping onto his bike and kick starting it to life even as Sam shouted for him to get off. The bike tore away before he could stop him and he wasn't going to shoot a kid. Instead, he told Eric to watch over them while he hopped onto one of the bikes. It growled to life and he gave it some throttle. The back wheel tore up the earth as he zipped away. He slalomed around headstones, his headlights washed over grave mounds and he hit a couple causing the bike to gain air. It had been a while since he'd been on a bike and this one kept making a funky noise as if it was about to quit on him. The guy he was chasing ducked his head and made his way onto the narrow road that cut through the cemetery. He was heading for the main exit when Sam decided to cut him off. He shot across a field of graves, went around multiple mausoleums until he burst out, turned the bike hard and peeled off down a short road. Trees and graveyards shot by in his peripheral vision as he rounded a bend that brought him down to the exit.

The kid was coming up fast. The dirt bike wailed as he gave it everything it had. The kid saw him but thought he could make the gate, and he might have if he'd gone a little faster except that was not what happened. The front tire of Sam's bike collided with the rear of the guy's bike. The collision was fast and brutal throwing both of them off.

Sam landed hard on the grass and rolled several times before coming to a stop.

He let out a groan and looked up to see the kid on the asphalt.

Luckily he was dressed in leather gear and wearing a helmet, if he hadn't he would have been torn up pretty bad. The bikes were a complete write off. They revved endlessly, the back and front tires mangled.

Sam rose to his feet and made sure all his limbs were intact before heading over to the kid. He was lying on the ground groaning. Sam crouched down beside him and placed a hand on his back. "You okay, kid?"

"What do you think!" he shot back. "You asshole. You nearly killed me."

Sam patted him on the back. "I think you'll be just fine. C'mon, get up."

He offered him a hand and after a minute or two of whining, he grabbed his hand and Sam hoisted him up.

"Why the hell did you run?" Sam asked.

"Why wouldn't I?" he said in an angry tone.

"Were you involved in the break-in?"

"No. I already told you that."

They walked back to the rest of the group who were now sitting cross-legged on the ground. Anna and Eric watched over them. It didn't take them long to get to the bottom of why they'd attacked Gene. According to them, he'd stolen gasoline from one of their homes and they were just trying to get it back when he came at them. Whether there was any truth to that, they would have plenty of time to tell the judge. Eric was still certain that two of them were involved in Richard's home invasion but they wouldn't admit to it. Someone wasn't telling the truth.

Chapter 10

Thorn bellowed out orders as he stormed back into the Launch Control Support Building. "Hector, get a few of the men and gather up sheets from the bedrooms, and head outside. There are two intake air ducts on the far side. I want you to cover them up, fill the insides of those tubes. I don't want any air getting inside, you hear me?"

Gripping his rifle, he nodded. "You got it."

He motioned to a couple of men and darted down the corridor to gather what was needed. Thorn and Dmitry entered the security control center, and got back on the phone again with the launch crew. He perched his ass on the edge of the table, a smile spreading on his face. The male lieutenant answered this time.

"Who are you?" Thorn asked.

"Lieutenant Douglas."

"Where's the woman?"

He didn't reply.

"Okay, look, I'm done playing around. This is your last chance to buzz us in."

"It's not happening."

"Look, this can get real hard for you. Those blast doors might be protecting you right now but they have one serious flaw."

"Which is?"

"They also imprison you."

"I hardly see that as a flaw."

"How's the air down there?" Thorn asked. "Must be stuffy."

There was a pause as if he was contemplating what he'd said and connecting the dots. When he didn't respond Thorn rocked back and grinned at Dmitry before continuing, "I'll admit, the two blast doors might be problematic for us but this one here, we'll get through it soon enough. When we do... I'm thinking that you could use a little less air down there. You know, maybe all that clean air is going to your head and not helping you think. So here's what I suggest. You open the doors, come on out and we will let you go. We have no need for you and by now you probably understand what we have in mind. So let's cut the crap, shall we?"

He waited for a response but got none.

"Okay. Let's play this the hard way. Enjoy the air while it lasts, as when we shut off the emergency generator, it's all you're going to have. Sure, those backup batteries are going to kick in and give you another six to eight hours of light and functionality, and you're probably thinking you are going to have to rely on that hand-crank stripper device to make some air but that only works if those two intake air ducts are functioning." He paused for effect. "That's right. You go ahead and think about that while we get to work on this door. Oh and if you have any thoughts on using the escape shaft, by all means, we look forward to seeing you."

With that said he hung up and motioned to a few of his guys to start working on getting through the first door. He didn't imagine it would take long. It wasn't like the two blast doors underground. It was just your everyday, run-of-the-mill security door. A pain in the ass but nothing they couldn't handle.

"How did you know about that?" Dmitry asked.

Thorn smirked. "C'mon man, give me some credit." He fished into his breast pocket and retrieved a folded up piece of paper. Dmitry took it from him and unfolded it. Inside was a site plan of the launch control facility.

"These fools made it available online." He clapped his hands. "Okay guys, let's get to work. We don't have long."

He exited the building to make contact with the second half of his team that were in a field over two miles away, preparing to dig down to the HICS cables.

* * *

Unsure if any of them were telling the truth, Sam took all four of the guys to the local police department. It was there that he got to witness first-hand the pressure the officers were under. The office was busy with numerous people being processed and booked into cells. He'd mentioned to the officer at the front desk that he wanted to speak to Chief Sanchez before he left. Like many others who were there to voice their concerns, file a complaint or try to get updates on those incarcerated, they were told to wait in line.

"I think we should come back," Anna said.

"Yeah, I second that," Eric said, gazing around at the crowd that filled the lobby. Many were waiting outside because there wasn't enough room. They'd had to elbow their way inside. Several people cursed at them and accused them of jumping the line. Sam sighed and nodded. They headed out and returned to Richard's home to assist in clearing up the house and securing it. The last thing Sam wanted was Richard staying with them. For a short while he even entertained the thought that the whole break-in was just something he'd concocted as a way to not be alone. He didn't dwell on it, instead he spent the next hour assisting Richard in bringing furniture back into the house while Anna gathered together paperwork that was scattered all over the home.

Outside in the yard, they had to work under the glow of the moon as the generator has been stolen. As he was turning over a recliner chair, he stopped and looked out into the woods.

"It doesn't make sense."

"What doesn't?" Eric asked, not even looking at him.

"Well you break into a home because you want to steal something."

"Nah, they wanted to send a message," Eric replied.

"But still, you're there and the place was loaded with food. The only thing they took was a generator."

"Everyone needs one."

"Sure but…" he trailed off. "When you saw the two figures, did they escape on foot or dirt bike?"

"On foot."

"So who was carrying the generator?"

"What?"

"Well, how did they get the generator out of there?"

Eric stopped what he was doing and shot him a glance. "Maybe there were more than two."

"But you only saw two."

"And I said there could have been more."

Sam nodded. "You see a generator in the cemetery?"

"Nope."

"Those things aren't light. The one Richard had was a good size. It would have taken at least two people to haul it out of here."

"Maybe they drove and left before the others did."

"Or maybe they weren't the ones responsible, just as they weren't responsible for stealing gasoline from Gene Landers."

Eric snorted. "You believe that?"

"They didn't strike me as the violent kind."

"You didn't see what they did to his face," Eric said. "Anyway, forget that, give me a hand." Sam took a hold of one end of the sofa chair and he took the other and they shuffled it over to where the window once was. They tossed it inside and returned to collect the rest. As they were walking back, Anna emerged from the house holding a stack of envelopes in her hand. She had this look of complete bewilderment on her face.

"Anna? What's the matter?" Sam asked.

Eric turned.

Anna held up the thick wad of envelopes. "He kept them."

"What?" Sam walked over and looked down at the envelopes. He instantly recognized them as those he'd sent to Anna. They were yellow, wrinkled by time and humidity but his nonetheless.

"There are even more inside. He had them stashed away in a box down in the basement. I can't believe it. You were telling the truth."

She looked back down and pulled out a birthday card. She opened it and read it aloud. Inside, the words told her that Sam had included some cash for her, and to enjoy her day but the cash was gone. She tipped her head back and squeezed her eyes shut and gripped the envelopes tight as if she was trying to get a grip on her emotions.

"All these years he told me you didn't care."

Eric approached. "He hid them from you?"

"Hid them. Intercepted the mail. Who knows? All I know is he never gave them to me and told me my father was a liar. And yet here's proof he was lying."

Sam swallowed hard and placed a hand on her shoulder. Eric looked at him and her, then dropped his head and walked away. Sam caught the expression on his face.

"You okay, Eric?"

He nodded but didn't say anything.

"Let's just leave," Anna said. "He can do this himself."

She didn't have to convince Sam, he told Eric they were heading back to the house. "You coming?"

"I'm gonna stay here if you don't mind."

"You sure?"

He nodded.

As they walked away, Sam did his best to talk Anna down from the ledge. She was seething. Once they made it back to the car, she stopped outside and looked at him. "Dad, I'm really sorry."

"It's okay."

"No, it's not. I went off on you back in Boston and…"

Sam walked back around the car and wrapped his arms around her. "It doesn't matter now. What matters is that you know the truth. I'd never give up on you, kid."

He kissed the top of her head and hugged her for a minute or two and then they got into the car and pulled away. It didn't take long to return to the house. Along the way Sam chose not to say anything. This was something she needed to deal with, but damn he couldn't wait to see the look on that asshole's face when she unleashed hell on him. If she was anything like her mother, Richard didn't know what was about to hit.

Anna was the first out of the vehicle. She jogged into the house, clutching the large wad of envelopes. They both walked straight past Mason, and he offered them a confused expression.

"She okay?" Mason asked. "You didn't piss her off again, did you?"

Before he could respond, Anna yelled, "Grandfather!

Grandfather!"

Her voice echoed in the house as she stormed into different rooms searching for him.

"I'm out the back," Richard replied.

Anna brushed past Amanda. Richard was sitting in a recliner chair, his head bandaged up, and he was smoking a cigar. Sam watched as Anna tossed the envelopes on his lap.

"You liar!"

Richard glanced down and then looked past her towards Sam as if he wasn't expecting to see him. "Hold on a minute, Anna."

"Why would you do that? Huh? All these years I've assumed my father didn't care. You allowed me to believe that he didn't give a damn. You even told me to my face that he had never sent a letter. You're a liar!"

He rose and groaned a little, reaching for his head.

"You've got this all wrong."

"Have I? It seems pretty obvious to me."

"Why would I keep them, Anna?"

"Because you didn't want me to see them."

"Then why didn't I burn them?"

Anna got this confused expression on her face. Sam shook his head. He knew where this was going. He was going to flat out lie again. It was just what he did. He was a master at it. He could turn a bad situation on its head in seconds. It brought him back to the night he handed over a video to Helen showing him in some seedy motel with Elizabeth. It didn't matter to her that he'd set him up or that Sam wasn't even aware of what was happening until it was over. He played on her emotions, and he was going to do the same thing again with Anna.

"I don't know. Maybe because you're sick and you wanted to be reminded of what you'd done."

"I kept them because your mother wanted to throw them out. I was planning on giving them to you when you were old enough. I forgot I had them."

For a few seconds Anna let his words sink in before she balled her hands then stabbed a finger against his chest. "Don't you dare blame her!"

"It's true." He looked over at Sam. "How the hell do you think I would get my hands on these?" He lifted one up and showed it to her. "It's addressed to her. I might know a few people in town but intercepting mail isn't something I dabble in. Your mother didn't want you to have a relationship with your father. And that's the truth."

"Yeah, I wonder why," Sam interjected.

Richard frowned. "You brought this on yourself."

"Go on, Richard, lie to her just like you did to Helen."

"I didn't lie, you goddamn piece of work. You were the one who cheated on her."

"You set me up."

"Prove it."

Sam gritted his teeth.

"Yeah, just as I thought. You can't," Richard said.

"Set him up?" Anna said. Her eyes bounced between them. "Set what up?"

Richard gave a smug smile, preparing to throw Sam under the bus. "Oh, he didn't tell you? Isn't that a surprise?" He looked at Sam. "Do you want to fill in the blanks or should I?"

Sam stared down at the ground, a wave of shame rolling over him. He knew he hadn't chosen to go back to that motel willingly. That wasn't him. But Richard was right, he couldn't prove it. It was for that reason alone that Helen kicked him out.

"I didn't walk away, Anna. Your mother didn't want me here."

Richard tipped his head back and started nodding. "That's right, try and play the victim card. The only victim, Sam, was Helen. You ruined a good marriage and walked away from Anna. And once again, you are ruining everything by coming back and sticking around and..."

"Shut up, grandfather!" Anna cried. She looked back at Sam. "What do you mean, set up?"

Sam breathed in deeply and brought her up to speed on what occurred that night, at least what he could remember, and then the fallout after a video was handed over.

"Couldn't have said it better myself."

Sam's jaw clenched, and one of his hands balled. He wasn't wiggling his way out of this, and yet Richard had already turned the tables when initially he was the guilty party.

"Is it true?" Anna asked.

"That was me on the video. Yes. But I did not choose to go back with her. I was drugged."

Richard threw up his hands. "Drugged. Please. Give me a break. Next he will be telling you that he sent you money in these birthday cards." Anna looked at her grandfather as he continued. "They're empty because he never sent you any."

Sam stepped forward. "That's bullshit and you know it!"

"Face the facts, Sam. You were a loser when you married Helen, and you're still a loser! Nothing is going to change that."

Sam lunged forward but Mason was quick to get between them.

"Whoa, hold on."

"Get out. Get out of this house now!" Sam yelled.

"I'm not going anywhere. If anyone should leave it's you!"

"It's my house. I will say who leaves and who stays," Anna piped up.

Both of them looked at her and she made a gesture to her grandfather to leave.

"But Anna."

"Leave."

"I'm telling you the truth. He's the one lying to you."

"LEAVE!" she bellowed in his face.

Richard stood there for a second or two, shaking his head. He shot a glance at Sam, sneered and quickly exited the house. The echo of the door slamming sounded so final. Sam reached for Anna but she shrugged him off and brushed past him. He heard her begin to sob as she hurried upstairs.

Tension hung in the air right before Chase said, "Damn, and I thought my family was screwed up."

Chapter 11

It took Thorn's team less than fifteen minutes to breach the door. Hector Richardson gave what was left of the door a hard kick and it swung wide, leading into a small grated area with an elevator. The emergency generator was housed in the Launch Control Equipment Building, a cramped room across from the capsule. It housed a diesel-powered electrical generator and additional equipment that handled environmental control for the Launch Control Center.

"After you," Hector said gesturing for Thorn to step into the tiny elevator. After, Hector pulled two steel gates closed and hit the button to take them down. While they didn't expect to encounter resistance, each of them were on the ready, gripping their rifles.

The elevator jerked to a standstill and they exited. Off to their left was a large mural on a blue wall of a nuclear missile with the letters USAF. The missile was breaking through a Russian flag. On the first blast door, which was closed, was the Domino's Pizza logo, except where it would have had the name of the company on the blue background, it had a white missile. Above were the words: World Wide Delivery In 30 Minutes or Less. Thorn chuckled. Only the military could be so contemptuous.

He turned to his right and walked into the open equipment building. Inside, air ducts snaked above them feeding through a wall of reinforced concrete and no doubt ending inside the Launch Control Center. To the right and left were diesel fuel storage tanks, and ahead was the generator.

"Okay, let's shut it down."

"But Thorn, we won't be able to get out. The elevator will stop working," Hector said.

He smiled. "They won't be in there that long."

He got back on the radio and checked with another one of his men to make sure they had blocked the air intake vents. It wouldn't be long before they would be gasping for air, overheated and desperate to get out. Eight hours, tops, and then the doors would open. They had all the time in the world. No help was coming.

Hector shut off the generator, and the sounds of fans whirring above them slowed and it went quiet. All the lights went out, and they turned on their flashlights.

"Now we wait."

"And if they choose to not come out?"

"They'll die."

"Let's hope they're not martyrs," Dmitry said.

* * *

The first thing Richard did when he stepped into his home was rip the bandage off his head. He was furious. He looked around and saw that some areas had been tidied while others remained in disarray. There was noise coming from the back of the house.

Richard darted into the kitchen and scooped up a knife.

He moved slowly through a set of open French doors into his living room, shining his light and trying to get a bead on who it was. He hoped, no, scratch that, he prayed that it was an intruder. He was in a foul mood and nothing would give him greater satisfaction than plunging a knife into some drug-fueled tweaker.

As he burst out into the corridor, a light flashed in his eyes.

"It's me."

"Eric?"

"Yeah, still clearing up."

He charged at him and slammed him up against the wall, quickly bringing the knife up to his throat. "Why isn't Sam dead?"

"I tried. I…"

"Don't say you couldn't do it."

"No, I did." He spat the words out. "I missed."

"You missed? You missed!" His voice rose.

"It was dark. There were too many. I didn't want to hit a kid."

He released his grip and Eric sank to the floor. Richard turned around and walked back into the living room searching for alcohol.

"This has gone too far, Richard."

"I'll say when it's gone too far."

"It's not right. She's already had her mother taken from her."

"And?"

Eric flashed a light in Richard's eyes. "What the hell has happened to you, man? You never used to be like this. Elly wouldn't have wanted you to do this."

"Well she isn't here now," he said continuing to root through his cupboards. He slammed them in frustration. "Not one *fucking* drop. He destroyed it all."

Richard got up and slammed his fist into the drywall, leaving a bowl-sized impression. He stomped into the kitchen and continued his search, then ran up the stairs hoping that the bottle he'd got for Christmas was still there, stashed away in a bag, tucked in a suitcase which contained anything that he didn't want out in the open. He got down on his hands and knees like a desperate drug addict searching for their next hit. He reached under the king-sized bed and pulled it out. The second he unzipped the brown suitcase, he smiled. Richard scooped up the bottle and clutched it like it was the last bottle on the planet. He unscrewed the top and chugged it down before wiping his wine-stained lips.

He backed away and pressed himself against the wall and looked around the dark, empty room. It reflected how he felt inside. There was nothing without Elly. She was the one good thing in his life. In the thirty-plus years they were married, she had always been there for him. Why she stuck around so long was a mystery. When he wasn't raising his voice, losing his temper with city council members, he was lost in his work. Just a few more hours, he would say. Weekends were a luxury. He worked harder than anyone in the city. And what did he have to show for it now? A large bank account that he couldn't draw upon, the power was off, the home was empty, his granddaughter hated him and the town was about to collapse.

As he sat there sipping on wine, Eric made his way upstairs.

He didn't say anything at first but just sat down beside him and they both stared out of the large window. A crescent moon hung in the sky over jagged mountains, the only light beyond that came from small fires still burning in the town.

"You know it's not too late to turn things around."

Richard chuckled. "Always the optimist, aren't you, Eric?"

Eric made a gesture for the bottle and Richard hesitated before handing it to him.

"I thought you'd given it up?"

"I have."

Richard laughed and handed it to him. Eric took a hard pull on it and gave it back.

"So what now?" Eric asked.

Richard glanced at his watch. "We still have a town hall meeting at eight."

"You're still going?"

"Why wouldn't I? The people need me now more than ever."

Eric shook his head. "Why do you do that?"

"What?"

"Try so hard to win the approval of people who don't care."

"Of course they care. If they didn't they wouldn't show up."

"They care about themselves. I meant you."

Richard rolled the bottle in his hand then chugged it. "If I don't have this. What do I have?"

"That depends on you. Why not be honest with Anna?"

"Because she'll never speak to me again."

"Did you hide the envelopes from her?" Eric asked. "Or was that Helen?"

He shot Eric a glance and smiled. "Does it matter?"

"It matters to Anna." Eric sighed. "Richard, I like you. I do. But... dishonesty only gets you so far."

"Is that so?"

He nodded. "Take it from a lawyer who has killed someone and covered it up, and tried to take an innocent man's life."

Richard turned and studied him. "Innocent? You think Sam is without fault?"

"I didn't say without fault. None of us are without blemish. I'm saying that he hasn't done anything to you."

"And you would know this because?"

"Because if anyone would have reason to bitch and complain, it would have been Helen. And in all the years after he left, she never once spoke badly of him. Sure, she was hurt by how things ended but she didn't resent him the way you do."

"I have my reasons."

"Well let's hope those reasons don't cause you to lose the only family you have left."

Richard looked over at him and downed some more wine. He just needed something to take the edge off before the meeting that night.

"So, do you still want me to kill him?"

"No. Leave it. Perhaps I'll do it myself, perhaps I won't need to. Maybe someone else will."

Chapter 12

Lieutenant Hart breathed a sigh of relief when the backup batteries below the floor kicked in and the lights and instruments on her console flickered to life. The only change was it was deathly quiet. The constant low drone of the air system was no longer in operation. She'd already been trained in what to do in the event of a nuclear attack, the commercial power was disrupted and the emergency power generators were damaged. It meant the launch facility would operate for another eight hours using the batteries built into the system, and they would have to use a device known as a stripper to create spare air. It was a hand-cranked device, which separated oxygen from potassium superoxide and depending on the number of cranks they gave it, determined how long they could last in the capsule.

There was meant to be a week's worth of air but that was based on the air intake working. Lieutenant Douglas was already flipping through the heavy, black-faced ring binder for the graph, which told them how many cranks it would take to keep them alive. The only problem was it relied on the intake ducts being clear and according to those above, it was now blocked.

Panic started to set in. They were now dealing in unknowns, completely uncharted territory. They weren't trained for this. While they figured the six-man security team had been compromised, she knew that as long as the air was working and they were behind the two blast doors they would be safe. There was supposed to be a week's worth of water and food under the flooring but that was only useful if they could breathe.

"Douglas, we need to get out of here."

"We can't leave this post."

"I'm not dying here."

"Get a grip, Hart," he said continuing to flip through the binder. He was composed, and she was far from it. Although she wasn't claustrophobic, she knew the odds of them surviving inside longer than eight hours were slim.

"Let's just head out the escape hatch."

"They already know about it."

Mia sighed. "So can they get in?"

"If they can find it, though the odds are low of that happening

. You see, when they deactivated the other 103 ICBM silos and eliminated them, they found that the ground had frozen and crushed the soil, essentially preventing anyone from being able to get out."

She stared back at him with a look of astonishment. "You're telling me we are trapped in here?"

"Not trapped. We could open the blast doors but that's not happening."

Mia slumped into her chair, her hands began shaking. She started breathing heavily and hyperventilating.

"Hey, whoa, whoa, slow down your breathing. We don't have much oxygen in here, we need to make it last."

"Last? You heard them. They are staying outside for the next eight hours."

"Yeah, they're trapped down here with us."

"But they're not trapped in a steel coffin. There is air coming down the elevator shaft. They can survive. We can't."

She buried her head in her hands.

"Hart. Don't you go losing it on me."

"You might not care if you live or die but I have a family. A kid. And they sure as hell don't pay me enough to put up with this bullshit."

"You signed up for this."

"I was assigned this."

"I meant you signed on to join the Air Force. You knew the risks."

"Of dying in battle, yeah. Not willingly allowing myself to die when I can open the door and walk out."

He snorted. "You think they're going to let you walk? The moment we open those doors we are as good as dead. They've already executed the security."

"You don't know that!" she replied.

"Of course I do. What, you think they're up there having a beer with them? Don't be so naïve."

Mia stood up and got close to him, and spoke through gritted teeth. "I'm not dying in here."

"I'm afraid we don't have any choice." Douglas turned and began cranking the stripper to purify the air, and essentially bring in new air.

"You're wasting your time," she said.

He turned the handle like a bike pedal, over and over again. "What they say they've done and what they've really done are two different things. I'm not going to sit by and do nothing."

Twenty minutes passed.

While Douglas continued to crank, she sat down, and was about to resign to her fate when the power kicked in, and the capsule flooded with air. She shot Douglas a glance and a smile flickered on her lips. They couldn't distinguish the sound of an elevator lifting, but they were sure they had retreated to topside as they felt the rumble of machinery kicking in. What did this mean? Had they given up? No. It was too soon. Something wasn't right. Why would they shut off the generator only to turn it back on again?

The answer came within minutes.

Mia reached for the phone as it began ringing.

"Hello?"

"Lieutenant. I'm going to go out on a limb here and assume you're the smart one. Am I right?"

Mia glanced over at Douglas who was wondering what he was saying to her.

"What do you want?" she asked.

"You married. Got kids?"

"What do you want?"

"That's the big question, isn't it? What do the people who have brought the country's grid down want? It's simple really. Payback. Revenge. What other reason has there ever been for starting a war?"

She shot back. "The blast doors won't be opened."

"Is that what he's telling you? You see, we can get in through the escape hatch if we wanted to."

"Then why don't you?" she asked.

There was silence on the other end, and then Mia

clued in.

"You don't want to damage anything that could protect you." She paused. "You want to protect yourself after you launch the missiles, don't you?"

"I knew you were the smart one." He chuckled. "Now it's simply a case of whether you wish to live or die. So will it be your colleague's life or both of yours? Well, lieutenant, what's it going to be?"

Chapter 13

Sam wasn't looking forward to this.

On the way over to the town hall auditorium they'd driven by multiple homes that had been consumed by fire. The fire service was out in full force and trying their best to put out the fires but not having much luck. Those with operational vehicles were diverted away from the chaos that had erupted in one of the neighborhoods. It was difficult to know what had caused it but multiple police officers were out in riot gear trying to control the situation.

Upon arrival they looked upon a knot of protesters jabbing signs in the air. NO MORE LIES. WE WON'T GIVE UP OUR FIREARMS. RESISTANCE IS BEAUTIFUL. One man held a red and white megaphone and loudly spewed hate for the city council. An angry crowd pushed forward trying to get into the building, ready to voice their complaints. According to a neighbor who was in attendance at the previous meeting, they were expecting the turnout to be as twice as many, and even more volatile.

Still furious at her grandfather, Anna chose to stay at home with Chase.

The car idled. They stared out into the darkness, a light rain was falling but the crowd didn't seem fazed by it. They were hyped up by one another.

"Well this looks like it's going to be a hoot," Mason said. "I think we should have brought our rifles."

Sam chuckled. "Was it like this in Oneida?"

Amanda leaned between the seats. "There were no town hall meetings. Things got out of control real quick. I'm actually surprised at how things have unfolded here. I figured it would be the same."

"Not everyone is a nutcase," Mason said. "Though I imagine Boston is a nightmare right now. Crime already high but take away the power and communication, shroud a city in darkness and all the rats come out to play." He turned to the others. "Well, shall we?"

They exited the vehicle and entered the ever-increasing swell of people. There had to be over a thousand in attendance, far more than the police department could handle. They'd already seen roughly ten of the twenty-five officers four blocks away trying to deal with a neighborhood riot, that didn't leave many to protect the town and oversee the evening's meeting.

"Stay close," Sam said gripping Amanda's hand and leading her through the crowd. It was a noisy scene with people shouting about a lack of food down at the shelter, and damage done to their properties. Others were complaining about sewage backing up, and an increase in looting. To someone looking on, it might have seemed premature, even unbelievable, and had this been the only town in the United States that had been affected, none of this would have been happening. However, with every town in the nation in a state of crisis there was one no one who could bring in additional resources, the Red Cross couldn't step in and alleviate the needs, and law enforcement couldn't receive backup from surrounding towns. They were on their own and quickly losing control.

The community was beyond pissed. They were outraged.

Sam and the others managed to squeeze into the building and find a place near the back; more officers inside turned others away. Sam had been counting the heads of officers and by his estimation most were here, which meant neighborhoods throughout the town were left unprotected.

"Man, this is wild," Mason said eyeing desperate faces.

"It might get worse," Sam said noticing a group of four guys force their way past officers trying to hold back the rest. One of their jackets pulled back and Sam spotted a handgun. Colorado allowed a person to open carry a firearm but they certainly shouldn't have shown up packing heat at a town hall meeting.

Chief Sanchez stood at the front of the auditorium, gavel in hand, smacking the podium. "Attention. Please.

Settle down. Order!"

It wasn't working.

That's when someone blasted a loud air horn.

Sam peered over heads and saw Richard Underwood appear in a doorway; in one hand he had the air horn, in the other a megaphone. "Enough!" he bellowed. The crowd quieted down to a murmur. "We are not savages," he said as he took to the podium and Sanchez stepped off to one side. "I understand you have complaints, questions and concerns and we are here tonight to answer them but let's make something crystal clear. We will not tolerate lawlessness. If you are here to argue, fight or incite a riot, leave now before you are arrested. Do I make myself clear?"

A few people cursed at him.

Richard blasted the air horn in their direction.

"You don't like it. Get out!"

He motioned to two officers to escort the unruly from the room. A task only made more difficult by those who felt they had a right to speak their mind. Seeing that he had the attention of the rest of the room, Richard adjusted his tie. He was still sporting the gnarly gash on his forehead and bruised lip but beyond that he presented himself well in a nice dark grey suit, with a red tie. Sam didn't expect anything less. The world could be falling down around him and he would still show up to work with his shoes polished and flashing pearly whites. He cared more about what people thought of him than those closest to him. Sam always believed that was the issue between them. It was never about him marrying Helen, or their disagreements over the way government was running the country. Sam just never fit into his ideals. He'd envisioned Helen marrying someone like Eric. Sam's gaze swept over faces until he spotted him near the door. He knew he would be there, a faithful follower of Richard, a man who worshipped at the altar of bullshit. He came across as a caring, all-round good guy but Sam had his doubts.

"Okay, first order of business. We are well aware that supplies are dwindling at the shelter. Please understand that what is being offered there has come from the good folks in town who wanted to support the community. The Red Cross, or the military does not supply them. We have very limited supplies. What remains is now being rationed out. You are all aware that wild game still exists so by all means feel free to hunt for what you need but know that in the coming weeks we may have to start monitoring how many deer, elk and bear one family can have."

"Weeks?" someone shouted out. A man from the group of four pushed his way forward. He wore a hunting cap and camouflage fatigues. "Are you telling me you expect this to go on longer?"

"Sir, we don't know how long this will last but we have to prepare for the worst."

He snorted. "And you expect us to allow you to monitor what we kill?" Several of his buddies started laughing.

"We are a community and we will help one another. This is not about helping yourself while others starve."

"If people don't hunt, they don't eat. That's not my problem."

"Where is your humanity?" a woman cried out.

"Oh sit down. Why should we have to go through all the trouble of hunting game to bring it back and share it with those who offer nothing in return?"

Richard was quick to jump on that. "No one expects you to receive nothing in return. We will continue to trade and offer items or services."

The guy turned and looked at the woman. "Hear that, darling? You might want to put some lipstick on and make yourself pretty. I'm sure we can find some way to trade."

The woman flipped him the bird and took a seat.

"That's enough!" Richard bellowed. "There will be rules."

"Rules. Best of luck imposing your rules on us. You've already tried to take our guns and that's not happening."

"Sir. What is your name?"

"Keith Boone."

Richard narrowed his gaze. "Howard's brother?"

"That's right."

"Where is Howard tonight?"

"Am I my brother's keeper?"

Richard shook his head in dismay. "Moving on! As I have said, you are free to hunt for food, though I would recommend you be mindful of others and help out as and where you can. Regarding water, there are the streams. Be sure to boil everything. Oh, and for those of you who are cooking outside, please take proper precautions with fire pits. The last thing we need is to have more homes on fire."

"Those house fires weren't started by fire pits," a woman yelled. "Someone lit them."

"And you know this because?" Richard said.

She looked nervously around as if searching for a face among the crowd. "I just know. That's all I'm saying."

Richard eyed her and then as he looked across the crowd his eyes narrowed as they fell upon Sam. Sam remained stoic and composed.

"Those of you who know about the fires, I would urge you to come and see Chief Sanchez or one of the officers at the end of the meeting. The protection of life in this community is our highest priority."

"I doubt it," a man said. "We got turned away from the hospital."

"I'm sure there was a very good reason. See me after."

"Fuck you," the guy said turning and squeezing through the crowd to leave.

"Pleasant," Richard said.

"I want to know why the power came back on and went off?" one of the four men yelled. "Rumor has it that we are the only town that doesn't have power."

"Sir, I can reassure you that is not true."

"Prove it."

"You can prove it yourself by traveling to any town in the surrounding area."

"Then how did it come back on?"

"Our government is working on solving the issue. I'm sure this is just one step they are taking among many."

"No it's not," a male voice cut through the crowd and everyone turned trying to pinpoint it. A tall, lean man in his early fifties pushed through. His face looked like it had seen better days; it was bruised and battered.

"Sir, I won't have you disrupt this meeting," Richard said.

The stranger continued. "You want answers?"

"We already have answers. Russia is behind it."

"No they're not."

Everyone was staring, and the crowd parted as the man made his way through. The front of him was covered in blood. He was wearing a blue shirt, black jeans and a thick brown leather jacket.

"And how would you know?"

Once the stranger made it to the front of the auditorium, he made a gesture for the microphone. He muttered something to Richard and he handed it over.

"Because I was the one who brought it down."

People looked at each other, a mask of confusion spreading quickly. Richard stepped forward and took the mic. "Okay, I think that's enough. Go take a seat."

The man wrestled with the microphone, not giving it back. "It was hackers and I was one of them."

In the crowd a young guy yelled, "Hey, I know him. That's Blake Dawson."

"Who?" several people asked, squinting at him.

The young guy, in his twenties, stepped forward. "Blake Dawson. He was thrown in prison back in the '80s for hacking."

Eyes turned to him and Richard stopped wrestling with the microphone. For the first time since the event had kicked off, there was a sense that perhaps they would get answers, even if everyone was skeptical that this man knew anything.

"Is that right? Richard asked.

He nodded. "I'm here to tell you that the power going down was just the beginning. They are about to start World War Three."

Several people started to laugh thinking he was joking. In all truth it was hard to buy into his spiel when he looked like he lived on the streets. First, his clothes were torn, he was covered in dried blood, and he looked as if he'd taken one hell of a beating. Second, who in their right mind would show up at an angry town hall meeting and admit to being behind the biggest attack on America? He had to have a death wish.

"Is it true?" Keith Boone yelled. "Were you behind this?"

Sam looked through the crowd and saw him sweep back his jacket, and place a hand on his gun. He didn't question what was about to happen next, it was obvious. These people were already fired up at the town's officials for minor issues but if they believed this man was responsible, they would kill him. Sam quickly pushed through the crowd making his way over, his eyes bouncing between Blake and Keith.

"I was forced to do it," Blake replied. "They killed my family and…"

Before he could finish, Keith yanked out a handgun.

"Get down!" Sam yelled motioning to those near the

podium.

Everything slowed in those final seconds as Sam lunged across two people and landed on Keith. They hit the floor hard, the gun went off and someone cried out.

On the floor Sam wrestled away the gun with a few sharp jabs to Keith's jaw as three officers descended. It was pandemonium as many people tried to flee, and others gathered around a woman who'd been shot.

The cops didn't mess around or ask questions, they grabbed both of them and slapped handcuffs on them. Sam felt a hard knee press on his shoulder even as Mason tried to intervene and tell them that he wasn't involved. Keith denied involvement and said the gun was Sam's.

"I didn't do it," Sam said.

"Leave him alone," Amanda shouted.

Around them a fight broke out between Keith's three friends and several men in the crowd. Two women jumped on the back of a cop who was trying to get a second cuff on Keith's wrist. All that could be heard was screaming and yelling.

Two more gunshots were fired from the front of the room and a calm settled over the crowd. Sam turned his head to see Chief Sanchez lower the gun in his hand. He took to the microphone. "Unless you want to spend the night in jail, you will back off and let my officers do their job!" The crowd moved away as Sanchez pushed his way through in a threatening manner. Hauled up by an officer, Sam glanced at Richard. He had this smirk on his face like he was enjoying every minute of it.

The cuffs bit into his wrists and a strong arm clamped onto his.

"You're under arrest, anything you say…"

They read him his Miranda rights as he and Keith were led away.

Chapter 14

Mia didn't care for Lieutenant Douglas but she wasn't going to kill him. After she hung up on the asshole, Douglas peppered her with questions. "What did he say? Is the generator staying on? Are they leaving?"

"No, he's not leaving," Mia replied with a hint of anger and frustration. She got up from the seat and eyed the escape hatch. Unlike the blast doors, once the escape hatch was open it really didn't offer much protection to the inhabitants of the capsule. It was designed for escape only, not for escape and returning.

Within minutes of the conversation ending, the power went off again and she slumped down.

"We might as well let them in," Mia said.

"Sure, why don't we just launch the missiles while we are at it?"

"It takes four keys, two of which are held at a different launch facility."

Douglas snorted. "I was being sarcastic."

"As was I." She breathed in deeply. "So what do we have to lose?"

Douglas walked back to the stripper and began cranking on it again. "I'm not opening the door."

"So you basically want us to die?"

Douglas slammed his fist against the counter. "We die either way. At least this way, we do it on our terms."

She laughed. "Our terms? They've been in control of us ever since they arrived."

"They're not in control now and I aim to keep it that way." Douglas gave up turning the hand crank and slipped into the single bed, rolled to one side and patted the empty space indicating he wanted her to join him. "Well if we're gonna die, do you want to…?"

"Hell no. Especially not with you."

He laughed hard and folded his arms behind his head. "I'm just joking."

Mia paced the room; her thoughts were with her child.

"I'm not staying in here."

"Yeah, you are," he replied without looking at her. "It's what you signed up for."

She casually walked over to the ladder which led up to a manhole cover, a few turns on that and sand would fall between the container and the capsule, and chains would stop the manhole cover from hitting her in the face. She would unbolt the chains, climb up a ladder welded onto the inside and go to the top where there was a small shovel for the last two or three feet of soil. She hadn't managed to get a few turns in when Douglas dashed over and pulled her back, throwing her to the floor.

"I told you. You're not going anywhere. We do this on our terms."

"Our terms or your terms?" she asked, throwing his words back at him.

"My responsibility is to stay in charge of this capsule, that includes you. I outrank you."

"Fuck your rank!"

Douglas folded his arms. "If we make it out of this, I'm writing you up."

"Oh go to hell!" she said, rubbing her side on the floor.

He stood below the manhole defiant. She would have thrown something at him if everything weren't secured. It was secured so that if a nuclear bomb hit the place, and the shock absorbers kicked in—the bed, microwave, and coffeemaker wouldn't fly across the room and potentially knock one of them out. The government had thought of everything except picking the right people. She sneered at Douglas. Mia felt like a penned-in animal.

He chuckled. "Even if you could make it out, don't you think he has someone posted outside that will kill you the moment your head breaks the surface?"

"I would rather die trying to escape than die in here like a coward."

Douglas walked over to her. "You might think it's cowardice but what I'm doing is for our country."

"You idiot. They're going to launch those missiles one way or another. You're not going to stop them."

"We already have," he said. He cupped a hand over one ear. "You hear that?"

She said nothing so he continued. "It's the sound of them doing nothing. They want in here to protect themselves after the launch, or did you think you were the only one who knew that?" he bellowed getting closer.

Mia saw her opportunity and took it. In a flash she reared back her leg and fired it at his face knocking him out cold. She scrambled across the capsule and climbed up to release the hatch. She shot a glance back at Douglas and kept twisting the handle until it gave way, and sand fell, some of it entering the capsule, the rest disappearing outside. Like someone trapped underwater swimming to the surface, she hurried up the diagonal ladder and pulled the shovel away from the side and jammed it into the hard earth to begin digging her way to freedom.

Beads of sweat dripped off her face as she put all her strength into it. It didn't help that it was hot inside the capsule and what little air remained was close to being gone. The earth was harder than she imagined. Maybe Douglas was right. Maybe it had frozen in the harsh Colorado winters and packed together. Small chunks broke away as she thrust the shovel at the dirt trying to pierce the earth. She thought she was making progress until she heard Douglas.

"Mia!" he yelled. Her nostrils flared and she sped up looking down to see him stagger into view. "You bitch!" He reached up and began to climb.

* * *

Back in Breckenridge, Anna was on her third glass of wine. She and Chase had convened in the kitchen. She was perched on a stool at the breakfast bar harping on about the nerve of her grandfather. In front of her was a large stack of envelopes from her father. She was going through them one by one. A glass in one hand, and an envelope in the other.

"It's like my whole life has been one big lie. How do I even know what is true anymore?"

Chase nodded, pulling a face. "I hear you. I said the same thing when my father came out a cross dresser."

She shot him a surprised look. "What?"

He burst out laughing. "I'm joking." She smiled and

gave him a nudge.

"You know, Chase I'm glad you came with us." She reached over and placed a hand on his.

"You are?"

"Yeah, I mean if we're all going to die…" she trailed off. His eyes widened and she cracked up laughing. "I'm joking."

She reached for the bottle and topped off their drinks and then slipped off the stool and went to find another.

Chase tried to change her mind. "We should probably stay clearheaded. You know what your father said."

"Oh I heard him. I'm just not sure if anything he says is true."

She returned with another bottle and Chase frowned. "But the letters. He wasn't wrong about that."

"No, but he said Elizabeth was just a friend."

"And he said he was set up."

"Who am I supposed to believe?" Chase stared back and then took a sip of wine. "Do I believe the person who's been around my whole life or a man I barely know?"

Chase shrugged. "What does your gut tell you?"

"It tells me to turn my back on both of them."

"But…"

"He still walked away, Chase."

Chase bit down on the corner of his lip. "But by the sounds of it your grandfather didn't make it easy for him."

"He could have stayed in Breckenridge."

"I imagine that would have been hard. Bumping into your mother, her family, and you."

She shook her head and took a big gulp of her wine. "This house doesn't feel the same without her. I just wish I could have heard it from her. You know, got her side of the story."

"Your mother never spoke about it?"

"She was very tight lipped. If I asked her a question she only told me the bare minimum. It was only in the last few months she started talking about him. I mean, can you imagine that? I lived the last eleven years acting as though I didn't have a father. That he didn't care. And that my mother didn't care. Only to find out that she still had feelings for him. That it was because of him she didn't date or marry anyone else."

"Not even Eric?"

She snorted. "Eric wasn't her type. He's a desk man. No. One thing I learned from her was why she loved my father. He was adventurous, spontaneous and had this wild streak in him. I think she was attracted to that because my grandfather smothered her while she was growing up. He never really let her live. You know?"

Chase nodded. "Then why did he send you off to school?"

"Maybe he wanted to surround me with people he admired. You know, Harvard types. They really are a different kettle of fish."

He sipped his drink. "You're telling me." He glanced around the room and then crossed to a cabinet. He picked up a photo. "This you?"

"Oh God, yeah, when I was like fourteen."

"You were attractive even then." He was quick to correct himself. "I mean, if I was fourteen I would have…" he trailed off and she smiled.

"Attractive even then? Does that mean…?"

He turned and headed back. "Okay, don't let it go to your head. We'll have a hard time getting you out the door."

She was about to say something when they heard a window smash.

Both of them froze.

"What the…?" Chase said.

Anna hopped off the stool and scooped up the Glock 22.

"Anna. Wait."

"I'm just going to check it out."

Chase collected Mason's rifle from the living room, made sure it was loaded and followed. Anna slipped down the corridor. She didn't fear anyone being able to break in because of all the bars on the windows but with the recent string of fires she was scared that someone might try to set the place on fire.

She spotted the brick on the floor in the dining room.

Anna peered through the peephole of the front door and saw several men fanning out. She didn't recognize any of them. Her mind shot into overdrive.

"Holy shit. Shit!"

"What? What is it?"

Chase took over at the peephole then backed up, a look of fear on his face.

Anna took only seconds to decide what to do. She hurried into the living room, brought up the Glock and began to fire multiple rounds out the window. One struck a guy in the shoulder.

"Chase. Check the rear."

Chase lingered in the doorway, frozen by fear.

She glanced at him. "Go."

He nodded and hurried away. Anna pulled back then scanned the room for anything she could put up to block the window. Nothing came to mind. She peered out again, it looked as if they had pulled back.

"How we doing, Chase?"

"Nothing so far."

* * *

Outside, shrouded by darkness, Howard Boone and Carl retreated to the end of the driveway, seeking cover behind a cluster of thick trees. After one of the rounds had torn Carl's shoulder and put him on his ass, Howard had rushed in and dragged him out.

"I thought you said the place was empty?" Howard bellowed.

"It was. Last week. She went into the hospital," Carl said, gripping his shoulder and groaning. "Am I going to die?"

"Not today, you idiot," he replied peering around the tree and trying to get a bead on whoever shot at them. Since going on a crazed spree inside Richard's home, he'd gathered together a group of Carl and Keith's friends and set them various tasks throughout the town. He knew the quickest way to bring an end to those looking to strip them of their guns was to distract them, make their job harder and ultimately break the town's morale. The community needed to see that no one was safe unless they were armed. Violence, disarray, and fires would spread throughout the city — it was the only way to drill it through their skulls, and dethrone city officials like Underwood.

He'd already seen how the people turned on the police after the six homes they'd torched along Lincoln Avenue and Main Street led to civil unrest. He glanced at his watch. Right about now Keith would be starting a riot down at the town hall meeting, that would keep cops at bay while he dealt with one more home owned by Richard.

It was common knowledge that Richard frequented a home on Peerless Drive. Howard couldn't think of a better way to get back at the man than to strip him of everything he cared dearly for. However, now they had an unexpected problem.

"You think it's her?"

"If it is, this is going to be a bad night for her."

There were eight of them crouched down in the tree line gazing at the house.

"I think I should get this checked out."

"It's just a graze," Howard said. "Suck it up."

"You call this is a fucking graze?" Carl yelled, taking his hand off to reveal a bloodied hole.

"It's your own fault," Howard said motioning to three of his men to head around the back. "I want in. You see anyone. Kill them." They nodded and took off leaving him to take the front with four others. He looked down at his hand that was cut up from trying to get past the barbed wire rolled around the property's fence line. He squinted at the window that was broken and saw a head peek around. He wasn't into negotiating, and he didn't have any fuel to burn them out.

He hadn't expected all the windows to be barred.

Carl winced. "C'mon, Howard, I need to get to a hospital."

"Shut up before I put another bullet in you," he said before darting out and motioning for the others to follow.

More rounds were fired as they zigzagged their way up the driveway and took cover behind a twenty-five foot fishing boat on a trailer.

"Okay, listen up. Chances are they've barricaded the doors, and we aren't getting through those windows unless…" he trailed off. "Paul. Bring up the Jeep. You got that winch?"

Paul nodded.

"We'll hook it up to the bars and pull them off. In the meantime, I want two men up on that roof. Take up the shingles; I want them to think we're heading in through the attic. That will distract them while Paul brings up the Jeep and I'll attach the winch to the bars."

Paul took off at a crouch heading to the vehicle.

Two of his men went around the side to climb.

Howard brought up his rifle and peered through the night vision scope.

He patted Terry on the shoulder. "Run across the driveway."

"But I'll get shot."

"No you won't. Trust me."

He was hesitant but he only had to remind them of what he'd promised — wealth, freedom from their criminal records and a place beside him when the town crumbled.

Terry jumped up and sprinted. Howard brought up the scope to his eye and focused on the window. *C'mon, c'mon,* he thought as he waited for the person to take the shot.

Sure enough he saw the hand come up.

But it was too late.

Howard squeezed his trigger, and a bullet tore through the hand.

Chapter 15

If the earth wasn't so solid, Mia might have escaped. Douglas reached up and clasped her ankle. Mia let out a scream, and used her other foot to kick his hand away. Douglas cried out. "Would you stop it. You're going to get us killed."

He stopped trying to get her for a second and leaned against the ladder trying to catch his breath.

"Killed? If we stay in here any longer we will die."

"And if we leave we have failed," he replied.

"Is that all you're worried about? Don't you have family?"

"Of course but they are only safe because of what I do here."

"Bullshit. You know as well as I do that they are going to launch those missiles one way or another. If they are responsible for taking down the entire grid, this is nothing to them."

"Well, I'm not letting you decide my fate."

"Likewise," she said before thrusting the shovel into the soil and trying hard to pull large chunks of it away. Douglas began to climb and this time he wrapped his arms around her calves and used his entire body weight to pull her away. Mia dropped the shovel in her attempt to hold on to the ladder. It disappeared out of view and clattered once it hit the floor in the capsule. "Shit!"

"Give it up Mia. You're not leaving."

He continued to climb up her, pulling at her green jumpsuit. Mia's fingers were slipping on the ladder, any second now…

She couldn't hold on.

They both slipped and dropped down into the capsule. Douglas let out a groan as she landed on top of him. She scrambled to get off, and scoop up the shovel again but he grasped her foot and she went knees first into the hard metal floor. Mia cried out and tried to crawl away from him but it was pointless. Douglas was bigger than her, and though he was older, he was more athletic and stronger. He was on her like a lion on prey. He flipped her over and in his crazed state backhanded her, knocking her unconscious.

* * *

Anna screamed in agony. Her cries were so loud Chase could only think the worst. He raced back into the room, his eyes bulging as he gazed upon her bloodied hand. His breathing sped up and he went into panic mode.

"Shit. Hold on."

He dashed out and began rooting through the kitchen looking for the first-aid kit.

"C'mon. Where the fuck is it!"

"Chase. It's in the living room," Anna shouted.

He sprinted in and spotted it on the coffee table. Within seconds he was back with her and yanking out Band-Aids, creams, and... bandages. "I got them. What else?"

"Get some water bottles from the kitchen."

He nodded and followed her instructions as she yelled out to him.

When he returned he nearly fainted from all the blood. He wasn't used to seeing that much. He didn't have a stomach for it. Other guys might have but not him. Anna talked him through what to do to clean and patch up the wound. The bullet had gone straight through her hand leaving a gaping wound. Several times he had to turn away as his gag reflex kicked in.

As soon as it was bandaged Anna sat back against the wall, tears streaking her cheek. Chase glanced at his watch. "Your dad will be back soon. They'll be back, right?"

She looked at her wristwatch. "Yeah."

It was the only thing that gave him hope. "Wait here."

"Where you going?"

"To see where those guys are." He placed Anna's handgun in her good hand. "I hope he taught you to fire with the other hand."

He didn't stick around for an answer; he darted out of the dining room, across the hall into the living room and peered out. He saw a few men dart around the side of the house, and heard what sounded like someone climbing. "No, no, no," he mumbled. This was the worst situation they could find themselves in. Trapped inside a home without anyone to protect them. He looked down at the rifle in his hand. "C'mon, Chase, pull yourself together." He felt like a complete wuss. He was the one that was meant to be able to rise to the occasion and yet everything inside him wanted to hide, run or give up. He glanced over at Anna who was groaning in agony. She kept putting down her handgun and gripping her hand.

"Don't pussy out now."

Thoughts of what his father said to him before he went to Harvard came flooding back in. His father was a hard-nosed businessman in California. Even though he had never been in the military or any career that might have hardened him, he didn't have patience for anyone who didn't have the balls to step up and take risks. It was how he'd built his real estate business. He was a get-the-job-done kind of guy who oversaw every aspect of his business from supervising workers to meeting clients. Nothing was below him and nothing was too hard.

"Only losers go to UCLA. Do you want to be a loser, Chase?"

"Harvard isn't any better, dad."

"Are you minimalizing my education?"

"No. I'm just saying. I don't have to follow your path in life."

"You're not. You're following your mother's. I don't think you have the balls to do what I do every day."

Chase gritted his teeth and took another look outside. He squinted into the darkness and saw two red eyes getting closer. What the heck? The sound of a Jeep's engine got louder as they reversed in. Bringing up the rifle he aimed at the rear tire and fired two times then unloaded several rounds at figures that darted in and out of trees.

Quickly pulling back he changed position, this time heading to the rear. He hadn't made it halfway down the hallway when the sound of glass breaking echoed loudly. They were trying to gain access in the back. Not seeing anyone, he raised the rifle and squeezed off a few rounds at the windows as warning shots. It might not prevent them from getting in but it would make them think twice about getting close.

He stood in the middle of the hallway, turning back and forth and firing rounds out the front and rear windows.

"Chase. Stop. You're going to blow through the ammo."

Right then he heard the sound of banging upstairs. He shot Anna a glance and then took off up the stairs heading for the second floor. It took only seconds to make sure that no one was coming through one of the bedrooms, but he could still hear the banging. It was coming from the roof.

Standing on the landing, he reached up and pulled the cord to gain access to the attic. No sooner had he done that than he heard a loud crash down below. He darted into one of the bedrooms and looked out to see the bars that had covered one of the windows were now in the driveway, attached to a chain. One of the men was unhooking it when Chase smashed the top window and fired at him. The single bullet hit its mark and the guy collapsed. The truck took off to escape the next flurry of bullets. As it did the chain caught a hold of the dead man and dragged his limp body out of the driveway. He pulled back as the window he was standing at came under heavy fire.

Not wasting a second, Chase shot back out onto the landing and pulled the ladder down. "Anna, check the window. I'll be down in a second."

He had to see what they were attempting to do.

Chase scaled up the ladder into the attic and shone his flashlight around. There were no holes in the roof but he could clearly hear banging farther down. He walked across the attic beams until he was beneath the banging. "All right, you assholes. Let's see if you like this."

He raked the rifle and fired multiple times peppering the roof.

Someone cried out and the next noise he heard was the

sound of a man yelling as he plummeted to the earth. Chase peered out the attic dormer vent and saw the same Jeep reversing in again. They were still driving it even though one of the rear tires was deflated. They were going to yank off more of the window bars.

The echo of gunfire could be heard as Anna tried to keep them back.

He listened again for movement on the roof but there was none. He figured they wouldn't stay there. Still, he fired a few more rounds in various places around the roof for good measure, just in case.

Anna yelled, "Chase, I need your help."

He double-timed it down to find Anna in the living room trying to shift a large china cabinet. The window and the bars were gone, a large opening offered the home invaders a way in. Anna was shouldering one side but not having much luck.

"Here," he said, hurrying over and tossing out all the plates and cups and pulling out the drawers to make it lighter. Once that was done, he fired a few more rounds out into the night to buy them some time while both of them pushed the cabinet across the room and shifted it into place to cover the window. As soon as the cabinet covered it, bullets peppered the wood. Both of them sank down as wood splinters spat over them.

Anna gripped Chase's hands as they waited for the onslaught of gunfire.

"Where are they?" Anna said glancing at her wristwatch.

"You ever see the movie *Butch Cassidy and the Sundance Kid*?" Chase said.

"What?" Anna said with a confused expression.

"There's this scene at the end where they're trapped inside this house without sufficient ammunition. Outside the Bolivian army was waiting for them."

She scoffed, and then groaned in pain. "Oh yeah, how did it turn out for them?"

"They both died."

"Great."

"Well, if it's any consolation some believe that isn't

how it really ended. Some swear they survived the ambush," he said.

"And some swear that Elvis was spotted on Mars," Anna replied as she dropped a magazine, and palmed in a new one.

"Why do you think they want in here?"

"What do you think? Bars on windows might protect us but they also send a message to criminals that perhaps we have something that is worth protecting."

"They don't teach that when they're telling you how to reinforce your home."

"Exactly." She looked over at him. "If we don't make it out of this—"

Chase cut her off. "Don't speak like that. We're not dying here."

"I'm just saying."

"Well don't. I'm already having a nervous breakdown as it is," Chase said before a smirk danced on his face. "How's your hand?"

"Painful."

He nodded and patted her leg. "Stay here. I'm gonna check the window in the dining room and see what these assholes are up to now."

He darted out and stayed low as he got close to the window. He peered out but couldn't see the truck, or anyone out there. Chase went to the rear of the house. Nothing. All he could hear was the sound of tree frogs and insects. It was dark outside, only a few clouds could be seen, and he could smell wood burning. Concerned they might try to smoke them out like the guys in Oneida, he dashed upstairs for a bird's-eye view of the property. Had they given up? No. They were out there. It seemed like a lot of work to go through to give up now. He was about to head back down when he saw the lights of a police cruiser. Had that drawn them away?

"Hey, hey!" Chase yelled from one of the shattered windows but his voice was lost in the wind. He hurried downstairs and bolted for the front door.

"Chase?"

"There's a cop at the end of the driveway. I don't see

the men."

He began unlocking the bolts.

"Chase. No!" Anna cried out.

He pulled back the door just in time to see one of the men dart out of the bushes. He came up behind the cop who was distracted by another guy, and shot him in the head. It all happened so quickly — Chase's yelling to get the cop's attention and the guy pulling the trigger.

He darted back inside and slammed the door closed.

Multiple rounds lanced the wood as he pushed home the bolts.

* * *

On the far side of town, Sam was being booked into the police station under the charge of disorderly conduct. "C'mon. I'm telling you the truth. The guy was packing. If I hadn't reacted you would have dead people on your hands," he said to an officer across the table from him.

"That's not what Keith said."

"You're taking his word over mine?"

"He's a local. What reason would he have to unload a

gun at a public meeting?"

"How the hell should I know? Surely you can check if the gun is registered in his name."

"With the system down, no."

"Well that's convenient. Look, speak with Richard Underwood. He's my daughter's grandfather. He'll vouch for me."

"Is that so?" The cop tapped his pencil against the table. "Actually it's because of him that you're still in here."

"What?"

"Yeah, our system might be down but we have paper records and he'd mentioned that you have a criminal record."

Sam frowned. "What the hell are you on about? I don't have a criminal record."

The cop scanned the table and pulled up a folder. He opened it and took out some paperwork. "Did you not damage his property, show up with a loaded firearm and make threats on his life?"

He turned the paper to show him.

"That was eleven years ago, and I didn't make threats on his life."

"But you were arrested with a loaded firearm."

"Yes but that's because he answered his door with a shotgun and threatened my life. You got this backwards."

The cop looked down at the paperwork, zigzagging it.

"Nope. No record of that."

"That's because he has the police force wrapped around his little finger." Sam sighed and leaned back in his seat. "Look, if you're going to book me. Go ahead. I'm tired of these questions."

"Don't worry, you'll get a chance to go before the judge and clear it up."

Sam didn't respond to that. How many officials in the town were in Underwood's back pocket? How many were reaping the benefits of knowing him? He should have just let Keith pull the gun. Maybe he would have killed Underwood.

"Don't I get a phone call to a lawyer?"

"Yeah, you do. It's just the phone lines are down so unless you know one—"

"Get me in contact with Eric Porter. He was at the meeting tonight. I want to speak to him."

Chapter 16

It was a hard tale to swallow. Richard Underwood watched from behind the one-way mirror as Chief Sanchez left Blake Dawson in the interview room after grilling him for the past thirty minutes. Eager to speak with the chief, he left the room and met him out in the hallway.

"Chief. A moment of your time."

The chief was getting updated on the situation that was unfolding in the streets. What had started as a small brawl, led to accusations being leveled at the police. They were certain if they hadn't darted out the back of the building they wouldn't have escaped with their lives. The crowd had taken on a mob mentality, and with their department divided and minimal assistance from people in the community, not even they could hold back the tide. However, Richard had prepared by having his driver pull up to the rear doors.

"What is it? I've got a riot we're trying to deal with right now."

"I heard what he said."

"You were in the other room?"

Richard nodded. He and Sanchez went way back. Richard had known him when he was just a young officer in the department. He'd pulled a few strings to help fast track his career, you know, put in a good word and create a few situations in town that enabled Sanchez to gain promotion.

"Do you believe him?" Richard asked.

He shrugged. "Hard to tell."

Richard grimaced. "If he's right, launching missiles would provoke Russia to go to war with us."

Sanchez breathed in deeply then puffed out his cheeks. "Maybe." He ran a hand around the back of his neck. "God, I am tired. You?"

"Exhausted."

"Look, I have a few things to take care of, would you mind having a word with Eric? Mr. Wade has requested him as his attorney."

Richard smiled. "Leave it with me."

"Thanks."

He turned and joined another officer down the hall and they both broke into a jog. The entire department was under an intense amount of stress. As the community of Breckenridge began to break apart, turn against each other and accuse, he knew it was only a matter of time before their town turned the way of those across America.

But that was no longer his fear.

Losing power was one thing. It was challenging but manageable.

Going to war with another country under these conditions would mean certain death.

Richard walked down the hall and entered the interview room. Blake looked up at him. His hands were in cuffs, and a chain went through the table to the ground. Richard took a seat across from him and studied his face. He looked down at the paperwork.

"My name is Richard Underwood, perhaps I can

help."

"You a lawyer?" Blake asked.

"Better than that. I'm the mayor."

Blake scoffed and shook his head.

"I heard what you said."

"You believe me?" Blake asked.

"I consider myself an open-minded person, Mr. Dawson. In light of the situation we find ourselves in, I don't see any reason why you would tell us unless of course you have mental problems or a death wish. Do you?"

He dropped his chin. "I used to think my freedom mattered. I'm not sure now."

"Regardless, the only thing I'm concerned about and that you haven't answered is this... can it be stopped?"

"The malware that took down the grid?" Blake asked. He nodded. "Yes but not from here. When it was done I was outside of the USA."

"And the Minuteman missiles, will... *Thorn* be able to launch them?"

"Yes. He will go through with it, if he hasn't already."

Richard took a deep breath and looked around the room before nodding. "Getting hold of the military would be difficult due to the circumstances we find ourselves in. F.E. Warren Air Force Base is almost three hours north of here on a good day, and Cheyenne Mountain Air Force Station is about the same."

Blake frowned. "You can't stop him. I thought I could but... what's done is done."

Richard leaned across and clasped his hands together. "You have family, Mr. Dawson?"

His chin dropped. "I did."

"Then you would understand what a man would do to protect those he loves."

He nodded. "Listen, I wish I could help stop the launch but..."

"Mr. Dawson," Richard said cutting him off. "You are familiar with how he would do this, are you not?"

"I am."

"Then you can help."

Blake shook his head. "This is out of my hands. For all I know he's already launched them. The best thing you can do right now is go home and be with your family."

"If he hasn't. Will you help?"

He shook his head and scoffed. "If it means getting my hands on that asshole. Yes."

Richard rose. "Hang tight, I'll be back shortly."

After leaving the room, Richard tracked down Eric. He was near the front entrance looking out at the crowd that had gathered. They were rowdy and many had damaged police cruisers by getting on top, and throwing bricks through the windows. He turned at the sound of Richard approaching. "Officers are doing their best to hold them at bay." He scoffed. "They're threatening to use rubber bullets and tear gas. Can you believe that? Did you ever think we would end up here?"

"Yes."

Eric's brow furrowed. "But you said…"

"Just forget what I said, Eric, and come with me."

"Where are we going?"

"To have a talk with Sam. He's requested you as his lawyer."

"His lawyer? But he didn't do anything."

Richard shot him a glance.

"Oh, right," Eric replied.

"Let me do all the talking," he said. They passed numerous empty offices. The department was practically a ghost town, every officer that could be reached had been summoned by Chief Sanchez to gear up and prepare for a riot. But that was the least of his troubles. He wasn't looking at the short-term issues but long term. If those missiles launched they wouldn't have to worry about riots, they would be looking at Russia retaliating and leveling the United States.

They entered the second interview room where Sam was in restraints.

"You bastard," Sam said the second he laid eyes on Richard. He struggled to get loose of his handcuffs.

"Settle down, Sam. You'll get out soon enough."

"You know full well that I wasn't responsible."

"I don't care about that. I'm here to discuss your freedom."

"My freedom?" Sam narrowed his eyes. "You arrogant son of a bitch." He lunged forward but Richard was out of reach.

"See, this is what I was I telling Helen. You are unstable."

"And you are out of your fucking mind if you think you control my freedom. Look outside, Richard. Can you hear that?"

The noise of the crowd had become loud. They could clearly hear the sound of rocks breaking windows. "You are no longer in control of this town, me, or anyone."

Richard's eyebrows rose. "You sure about that?"

Sam's eyes bounced to Eric. "He has you on the payroll, doesn't he?"

"Eric is here because you requested him."

"Then maybe you can leave," Sam sneered.

"Eric works for me."

Sam laughed and sat back. "Of course he does."

Eric looked at him as if he wanted to say something but he didn't. He wouldn't. He didn't have the balls to. There were few people in the town that did. It wasn't that Richard was an intimidating man, but his reputation preceded him. Those that had tried to go against him were quickly dealt with in various ways, most of which included a high-priced lawyer.

"Why are you here, Richard?" Sam asked.

"I have a proposition."

"Like the one you proposed to me the week before you set me up?"

Richard snorted. "Still living in the past, aren't you, Sam?"

"And you're not?"

Richard remained standing, he didn't trust Sam but on the other hand he had to, their lives depended on it. "One thing you are right about is that we are losing control of this town but that is not our biggest problem. The men responsible for bringing down the grid are going to launch Minuteman missiles at Russia. I don't have to explain to you what the repercussions will be if that happens."

"And?"

"And we have very limited options for stopping them."

Sam shrugged. "I don't see how any of this matters to me."

"It should. Anna's life would be at stake. It would be a terrible thing to lose her after such a beautiful reunion, don't you think?"

Sam shook his head in disbelief. "Oh my God, man. Can you even hear yourself?"

"I'm putting together a team who will go with Mr. Blake Dawson to the launch facility not far from F.E. Warren Air Force Base. I want you to go with them."

"And why would I do that for you?"

"Because you care about Anna. It's not for me. Well, I should correct that, of course I will benefit if you're successful but that's not the issue here. Of course I won't leave it entirely up to you and I'll attempt to get in contact with the military by ham radio but right now you are the only person I know that is trained to lead a team of people for an operation like this. Now I can arrange for…"

Sam started laughing. At first it was just a chuckle then he broke into a full belly laugh. Richard looked at Eric and then back at him.

"Stop it," Richard said in a calm tone.

Sam continued to laugh until there were tears rolling down his cheeks.

"I said, STOP IT!" Richard leaned forward and banged his fist against the table. In an instant Sam lunged forward and grabbed him by the head and bounced his face off the table. He released him then rocked back and laughed.

"Damn! That has got to hurt! Ooh, I hope you've got a good dentist on the payroll."

Sam continued laughing uncontrollably.

Richard's eyes watered and he winced in pain, as he cupped two hands over his face. Blood gushed down into his mouth, one of his teeth was chipped, and his lip was busted up. He turned and stormed out of the room cursing loudly. Eric followed him down the hall and into the bathroom. Richard yanked multiple brown paper hand towels and went over to the mirror and looked at his face. *Bastard.* He'd broken his nose.

"Are you okay?" Eric asked.

"Does it look like I am?" he spat back.

"You should really hold your head back. It helps stem the bleeding."

Richard scowled at him and then did exactly that. He slumped down onto the tiled floor and shook his head. He should have known trying to reason with that lunatic wouldn't have ended well.

"You want me to go and speak to him?" Eric asked.

He turned. "Would you?"

"Just tell me what you need."

Richard placed a hand on his shoulder. "You're a good man, Eric."

* * *

"They killed a fucking police officer!" Chase said.

"Get a grip, Chase." Anna got up and made her way over to him. The pain was excruciating. If she didn't get to a hospital soon she was liable to die of infection or a loss of blood. She felt nauseated and dizzy and for a second she lost her balance and stumbled into the wall.

"Anna."

Chase rushed over and slipped an arm around her shoulders to support her. "We need to get you out of here. Screw it. They can have whatever they want."

He guided her to the rear and placed her against the wall.

"Yeah, it's the getting out part that's going to be a problem," she said. Chase went over to the window. He couldn't see anyone out there but that didn't mean they weren't there. They'd killed two of them and injured another. Maybe now what they wanted in the house was them.

He swallowed hard and checked the ammo for the rifle.

"Look, we're gonna have to make a run for it," he said.

"And how do you suggest we do that?" Anna asked.

Chase rushed to the front of the house and peered out the window. He could see them preparing the chain on the back of the Jeep to do another window. If he only knew how many there were, he could figure out what they were up against. He had to assume there were more, in which case they needed another way out. The problem was with bars on all the windows they had pretty much imprisoned themselves.

He returned to Anna. "Besides the front and back. Are there any other exits?"

"The garage, that's it."

"That can't be it."

He paced the room for a minute or two, occasionally looking down the hallway expecting them to burst into the house at any moment. In the attic there was an eyebrow dormer. It wasn't very large but if he kicked it out, it offered an alternative means of escape. He would have to keep those on the ground distracted while she slipped out and made her way down onto the roof of the garage.

"Come with me," he said.

"Where are we going?"

"I'll show you."

He led her upstairs and they climbed the ladder into the attic. Small bands of moonlight filtered through the bullet holes in the roof. He led her down to the dormer.

"Listen, I'm heading down. I'll distract them. Wait until you hear me firing before you break the vents. Slip out, keep your head down and head to the west, towards your neighbor."

"And what about you?"

"I'll follow but one of us has to keep them occupied."

"Chase."

"I'll follow, just do as I say."

With that he turned and exited the attic. No sooner had he made it halfway down the stairs than he heard a loud crash coming from the living room. He moved fast, in the hopes of cutting them off before they entered. Sure enough as he came around the corner, one of them was crawling in through the opening. They'd pushed over the cabinet. Chase brought the rifle up as the man glanced at him. A look of shock spread on his face before a bullet tore through his skull. He fired another four shots near the window to keep the others back.

Go Anna, go, he thought as he took a knee and unloaded a few more rounds to distract them. Directly behind him he heard the bars being torn from the house in the dining area. Chase darted across and peppered the walls around it. He knew it was only a matter of minutes before they burst through one of the windows.

Chase unloaded a magazine and palmed the last one he had into place. Then he ran up the stairs, taking two steps at a time. Sweat poured off him. His fear had reached new heights as he made it into the attic. He reached down and pulled up the ladder to buy himself some time. Once the attic door was closed he turned and ran towards the side of the house. Anna was gone as were the vents. There was no time to think about the threat of a gunman on the roof. He slipped out the hole and made his escape.

Chapter 17

Mia gasped as she bolted upright. Her eyes bulged as she looked around her, fear shot through her. Douglas was casually perched on the console with his feet on the seat. He was rolling a stress ball around in his hand and observing her through slitted eyes as if trying to decide what to do with her.

"Welcome back."

She scrambled back from him, leaning against the blast door.

He laughed. "I'm not going to hurt you."

She reached up and felt the side of her face. It stung and felt slightly swollen.

"Oh, about that. Sorry but it was necessary. You didn't really give me much choice." He stopped rolling the ball around. "You know, going batshit crazy last night."

She frowned. "It's morning?"

"Yes, and that's air you're breathing." He hopped off

the seat and tapped the air vent. It let out a tinny echo. She instantly became aware of the steady drone of air being pumped into the capsule. She glanced up at the twenty-four hour clock on the wall. It was just after five in the morning. Her brow pinched together. It didn't make sense. They should have been dead by now.

"How?"

"Like I told you, before you rudely kicked me in the face." He glared at her letting the words sink in. "They're not going to kill us. We're the only ones who can open that door. And they won't come through the escape hatch because they don't know where it comes out. And if I'm right and I believe I am — the reason they want in is to protect themselves after launching those missiles so if they take a cutting torch to that blast door they are jeopardizing their own safety. Again, like I said, the safest place for us is in here."

"How long has the air been on?"

He shrugged. "Three, maybe four hours. Four I think. They turn it on when he wants to communicate. He phoned several times while you were out cold. Strangely, he wanted to speak with you, not me. You wouldn't by any chance know this individual, would you?"

She scowled at him. "No. Why would I?"

"I don't know. The way you acted all irrational yesterday. Got me thinking."

"About?"

"Ah it's nothing. Just mulling things over. Oh, by the way..." Douglas walked over to the hand crank stripper and turned it. "It's working. How about that, eh?"

She frowned.

"Don't look so surprised, Mia. They obviously didn't think this through. By my estimation the air has been running for the last..." He looked at the clock again. "Six hours, off and on. But the last time they turned it on was four hours ago. They haven't switched it off in four hours. You know what that means?"

"I'm sure you'll tell me," she said rubbing her jaw.

"I think they're gone."

"No they're not," she replied.

Douglas walked over and crouched down just out of reach. "Mia. If you wanted to launch missiles would you wait around for us to open the doors? There is too much on the line to wait. I think they've changed their plan." He got up and went over to the door. "I just wish we could see outside. You know, to be sure."

"They're not gone," she said. "They're waiting for you to open up."

He looked back at her. "And why would we do that? We have enough food and water to last a week in here. They're pumping in air. All systems are operating."

Mia shook her head and rose to her feet, she lifted up the flooring that covered the additional supplies of food and water. "You sure about that?" she said. Douglas looked over and his eyes widened.

"Where is it? Where are the supplies?"

She shrugged. "Your guess is as good as mine. I figured it was in there."

Douglas dropped down to his knees and pulled up the next panel. It was empty; he did the same with the next three panels.

"No. No. That's impossible. They always have this replenished."

"Have you ever looked under here?"

Douglas looked at her, total shock setting in. He went over to the mini fridge and looked inside.

"Yeah, and we have practically worked our way through what we have," she said.

"You knew about this?"

"No," she said. "And I'd appreciate you not accusing me."

He shook his head unable to grasp the gravity of their situation. She could hear him mumbling under his breath; something about they always kept it stocked, didn't they? The truth was no one had checked. At least they hadn't. The likelihood of them having to use it was slim to none. And any food that was under there might have been removed due to expiration dates. It was also possible that they had every intention of replacing it but the timing of the power grid going down may have interfered — or perhaps when they were talking about government cutbacks this was what they meant.

Douglas stumbled back, and slumped to the ground.

Now she understood why he wanted to stay inside, why he was acting so nonchalant about it. He thought they could survive at least another week.

"We need to head out," Mia said. "Or we will die."

"No, we have air. If they wanted us dead they could just shut off the air and leave."

"Then they would be trapped down here with us. That's why it's on."

"You don't know that. For all we know, a few of them could be down here and the rest topside."

"It's been four hours since they called. I'm getting out of here."

"No one is leaving," Douglas said.

Mia sighed. "Let's at least open the first door and head out onto the bridge. Maybe we can hear them banging around."

Between the two blast doors was an area where the

shock absorbers had been installed. Often, when they had the door open to let in the cook, or next shift change, they would hear the elevator and security.

He looked back at her and for the first time since this whole thing had kicked off, he agreed.

* * *

After escaping from the house, they had no other choice than to head north towards the town of Frisco. It wasn't just that St. Anthony's Hospital was there and Anna needed medical attention but the streets in Breckenridge were chaotic. At first they were going to head for the town hall but several riots had erupted, and many businesses and homes were on fire. They'd seen a group of ten people attacking two police officers. Tear gas was fired into the angry mob but it didn't stop them. Black smoked drifted across the roads, and the threat of being attacked made it too risky to stay.

Instead, they walked for three hours only stopping a few times to get water from the stream and to wash her hand. Several times Chase had suggested they stop at someone's home and see if they could get a ride but Anna wouldn't risk it. The only thing pushing her on was the thought that if she didn't get treated she would die. She had no idea that someone could survive a bullet wound to the hand. All she saw was blood and lots of it.

They arrived shortly after two in the morning.

Police officers outside the hospital saw them stagger across the parking lot and hurried out to assist. She fell into their arms and passed out.

Now as her eyes fluttered open, she awoke to see the sun rising above the Rockies. The curtains were partially open and she could hear the EKG monitor beating steadily. Her head turned to see Chase asleep. He was sitting in a chair beside the bed, one hand clutching hers and his head resting on the sheet.

She groaned and he looked up.

"Hey," he said scooting forward. "How you feeling?"

She pawed at her eye. "Like crap but rested."

Chase smiled and gave her good hand a squeeze. "Can I get you a drink?"

She nodded and he left the room with a paper cup.

Anna stared at her room. Eleven days and the hospital was still operating. Despite the riots they'd witnessed the night before, it was good to know that some semblance of order still remained.

* * *

Mason stretched out his body, and looked across at the others inside the cramped cell. Due to the riots in town they'd seen an increase in people being jailed overnight and without enough room to hold them, a cell that was usually meant for one person now held five. He was in with Keith Boone, and three other nasty looking individuals. Two of them had arrived sometime in the night, drunk and belligerent. For a short while he thought he would have to defend himself but fortunately that wasn't to be. After they banged on the door and cursed at the officer who'd tossed them inside, one of them slumped down and fell asleep while the others spent the next hour curled over the only toilet throwing up. As he awoke that morning, the smell of vomit and piss dominated. There was only one bed in the room — if it could even be called that — and Keith Boone had taken that, so Mason had slept in the corner, using his jacket as a pillow.

Rubbing his eyes he looked down at the two drunks and the gnarly pool of vomit in the toilet. "Oh God. Gross." Keith Boone was already awake and sitting with his back against the wall and his arms wrapped around his knees. He glanced up at him but didn't say anything.

Mason stepped over one of the drunks and banged on the door. He was still pissed that they'd thrown him inside, citing disorderly conduct. Amanda had been taken to a different cell for women.

"Amanda. You there?"

A few seconds passed before she replied.

"Yep."

He dropped his head against the door and closed his eyes.

"We'll be out of here by the end of the day," Keith Boone muttered. "There's no way they can keep us in these kinds of conditions, especially on these bogus charges."

"Bogus?" Mason turned scowling at him. "If it wasn't for you we wouldn't even be in here!"

"Hey, I didn't do shit."

Exhausted. Hungry. Pissed off. Mason lunged at him and fired a punch to his jaw. Keith hit back, throwing one into his stomach. He stumbled back, grimaced and pressed forward and yanked him off the bed, dragged him over to the toilet and forced his head down inside. There was a good chance he might have drowned him in that vomit had it not been for the clunk of a lock, and the door swinging open.

An officer jumped into action, grabbing Mason and dragging him out.

Before the door slammed closed, Mason saw Keith's face covered in vomit. He chuckled, and flipped Keith the bird. Keith spat out something nasty from his mouth, and began protesting but the cell door quickly muffled his cries for mercy.

"Mason."

Mason turned to find Sam, and Eric nearby.

"Sam." He crossed the walkway and gripped him on the shoulder. "You okay?"

"I'm fine but you look a little shaken up."

Once the officer was done locking the door he turned and slapped Mason on the arm. He stuck a finger in his face. "Buddy, you're lucky. Believe me."

With that said he strolled over to another cell and released Amanda.

After a short reunion, they were led upstairs to be processed and released.

"So they understood?" Mason asked.

Sam shook his head. "Not exactly."

* * *

It didn't take them long to receive back their personal belongings. As they stood waiting for the officer to process them, Sam looked out the front doors. A deep rising sun shone through the windows. Smoke filled the sky, and streaks of red and yellow stretched over the town.

"What happened last night?" Sam asked.

"Don't even ask," the officer said sliding an envelope across the table. Sam took it and emptied out his watch, twelve dollars in cash, his wallet and a pack of gum. He turned to walk out and Mason fell in step.

"You want to tell me what's going on?" Mason asked.

"I... I have to do something. I need you go back and keep an eye on Anna."

Mason looked back inside the department and saw Blake Dawson being released.

"It's related to him, isn't it?"

Sam nodded. He really didn't want to get into it with them because he didn't want Anna to worry. There was a very good chance they wouldn't see each other again and he felt the less he said the better.

Mason pestered him. "Sam, where are you heading?"

He sighed and stared at the charred bones of vehicles. The street was a mess; broken glass on the ground, fire burning inside vehicles, paper covering the ground like huge snowflakes, buildings covered in graffiti and protest signs scattered everywhere. While there were still some people on the streets most had retreated to sleep off whatever state they were in. Outside, three armed officers kept watch as he waited for Blake Dawson.

"Sam. What do you want us to tell Anna?" Amanda asked.

"I don't know." He had given a lot of thought to it over the night but none of it seemed reasonable. He could have told the truth but then she would worry, and he couldn't guarantee he would be back. Sam thought back to all the operations he'd done over the years. Back when he was married to Helen he would tell her he was going overseas but he would never tell her the specifics of what he was doing. She didn't need that troubling her mind; she had enough to deal with raising Anna.

Blake came out and rolled his head around.

"You must be Sam?" he asked.

Sam nodded.

"Blake Dawson."

"I know," he said. "Where are the rest?"

He looked over his shoulder. "Officer inside said they'd be out soon and to wait here."

"Sam. I'm going with you," Mason said.

"No, I need you to stay. Please. Keep an eye on her."

"All right."

Amanda gave him a hug and held on a little longer. "Stay safe," she said in his ear before breaking away and walking off with Mason. They looked back for a second and then disappeared into the black smoke drifting across the road.

"You know I'm beginning to understand her," Eric said. He'd been standing nearby looking out at the town that was just beginning to come to life. Although Sam was confident that there was little the police could do to him, being as it was his word against Keith Boone's, he'd agreed to the arrangement of going with Blake on two conditions. One, Richard had to admit to Chief Sanchez that he'd lied about Sam attacking him on that night years ago. It wasn't a matter of humiliating him though that did give him great satisfaction to see him backtrack on his original statement — it was a matter of principle, he didn't want a criminal record. If he was going to stick his neck on the line, he wanted any record of his past to be cleared. Two, they were to attempt to get a message via ham radio to the military to provide the coordinates and update them on the situation. As much as he was used to working in small teams to achieve an objective, he wasn't stupid. Having backup from real professionals was critical.

"Understand who?" Sam asked.

"Helen. The way she spoke about you. I uh… was planning on proposing to her when she got out of surgery but I have a feeling she would have said no." He turned to him. "She loved you, Sam. That's for sure."

Sam was about to say something when the door behind them opened. An officer stuck his head out and motioned for them to follow. "The chief is going to brief the team, if you two want to step inside, we'll get you geared up. They're leaving in ten minutes."

Chapter 18

As Mason turned the bend in the road leading into the neighborhood, he saw smoke rising. A thick billow of black smoke drifted across the trees and blocked the view of the home. At first he thought it was the woodland that had caught on fire, as they'd passed numerous areas that had been burned to the ground. Mostly it was vehicles that had been set ablaze, and businesses but there had been far more destroyed since yesterday.

He squinted, and then his jaw dropped.

Mason gave the engine some gas and accelerated. The derby car couldn't go fast enough. Panic washed over him at the thought of the home being destroyed or worse — Anna and Chase attacked. They'd already seen a few people lying face down in the streets, those that had fallen under last night's riot. No ambulances had shown up nor would they. From the little he'd gleaned from an officer before leaving the department — the previous night had been the worst they'd ever faced. While not all the hate was directed at city officials, the fights on the streets had caused them to retreat and barricade themselves in the department.

"It's not the house," Mason said trying to reassure Amanda. "We took precautions."

Amanda nodded but it was clear she didn't buy it.

He thought of all the time they'd put into securing the property. The barbed wire, the bars on the windows, the signposts, and the additional locks, all of it would have deterred intruders. Wouldn't it?

Mason yanked the wheel hard to the right and veered into the driveway that was shrouded by trees. The very second he pulled up, he slammed on the brakes, took the Glock from the glove compartment, gave it to Amanda, grabbed the AR-15 from the trunk and approached. Only the right side of the home had been destroyed. As a good portion of it was made from stone, the damage appeared to have come mainly from the inside.

He walked around the window bars on the ground and

looked at the front of the home. Two of the windows had been torn away. There was a chain nearby with a rusted hook on the end. The walls were peppered with rounds and hundreds of spent shells littered the ground. Mason glanced at Amanda and back at the house. Cautiously they approached and looked through one of the open windows. It was a total disaster inside. Furniture destroyed, and the walls torn up by gunfire.

Mason threw up a hand. Amanda stopped walking. They listened carefully but there was no sound. Confident that no one was inside, they entered. Glass crunched beneath his boots as they walked into the hallway. Quickly they cleared each of the rooms on the main floor and second floor. It was like someone had gone berserk with a sledgehammer and an automatic rifle. Every window was shattered causing the cool wind to blow the drapes around.

"Anna? Chase?" Amanda yelled.

On the landing, the attic door was down. Mason went up and peered inside. At the far end he saw the vents had been busted out. Had they escaped? Or was that how the intruders entered? No, it was a good height up from the garage roof. They would have needed a ladder. However, it was possible that Chase and Anna had dropped down from there.

"Anything, Mason?"

"Hold on a second."

He went up and crossed to the far end and looked out. Mason stared up at the ceiling and crouched down and picked up a shell. He rolled it between his fingers. Mason went back to the window and looked out before heading down to the landing.

"What did you find?" she asked. He handed her a shell and walked downstairs and into the backyard. That's when he spotted a dead guy near the flowerbed. A large pool of blood was around his waist, and head. He crouched down and looked out towards the woodland. *Where did you go?*

"Mason, what are you doing?"

He went back inside and noticed blood near one of the

windows at the front of the house, a first-aid kid lying open nearby and droplets of blood leading up the stairs. He went back up again. He hadn't noticed it the first time around. He took a flashlight from his pocket and switched it on. Even though it was daytime, inside the home it was still dark. He followed the trickle of blood up the steps and into the attic. At the far end he noticed blood on the frame of the window.

When he came back down for a second time, he was lost in thought. "I think one of them was injured. Where would you go if you were shot?"

Amanda didn't even have to answer.

They hurried out of the house and got back into the derby, and took off in the direction of the hospital.

* * *

"I don't understand, Thorn. What the hell are you playing at?" Dmitry said.

Thorn was on the radio talking to one of his men several miles away who had dug down and was ready to tap into the HICS cable. He put up a finger to let Dmitry know that he would answer that in a second.

"No, don't make the connection yet. Good work. Just hang tight."

Static came out of the radio and he looked up at Dmitry. They were sitting inside the security control center and he had his feet up on the table. He placed the radio down and took out a pack of cigarettes.

"Take a seat, Dmitry. Everything is going to plan."

He tapped out a cigarette and lit it.

"We should have launched them by now."

"And then we would have thirty minutes to find cover." He shook his head. "Don't be stupid. We've run into a bit of a hurdle. It was to be expected. Have a little trust, my friend."

Demitry replied through gritted teeth, "They're not coming out."

"They'll come," Thorn said confidently.

"It's been over six hours since you turned the power back on. I don't understand. I thought we were going to cut off their air supply?"

Thorn blew out smoke from the corner of his mouth. It spiraled up and caused him to squint. He tapped the side of his temple. "Oh my God. Did you not listen to anything I told you earlier?"

"Don't treat me like an idiot."

"Then don't act like one. It was a ploy to get them out. First off, don't act as if this is my fault. If your buddy Hector had not shot the guy here in the head," he said pointing to the security officer who'd been manning the security control center, "we wouldn't be in this fucking mess." He took another hard pull on the cigarette. "So we have to adapt. This launch crew obviously has a martyr complex and they're willing to go down with the ship. In which case leaving the air off would not benefit us being as we need them alive to open the fucking door."

"Why don't we just using a cutting torch?"

"Um. That's a great idea. And then when Mother Russia drops its nuclear bombs, what are we going to use to seal up the hole? Scotch tape!" He rolled his eyes. "My God, I'm surrounded by idiots."

Dmitry got real close. He was a burly man with a bald head, icy blue eyes, and a scar down the side of his forehead from a bottle attack in a bar. He was wearing a black bomber jacket and tight blue jeans. Like many Russians, he had a no-nonsense attitude. Thorn had met him a long time ago on one of the many hacker forums. Only three out of the ten men assisting them were his friends, the rest he'd met through various acquaintances, some were known from hacker groups. Contrary to what most thought, not all hackers had the same skillset.

"You promised me!" Dmitry said.

"I promised nothing. My goal was to bring the grid down. You were the one who wanted to launch missiles. All I said was that it could be done."

Thorn rose and straightened. He wasn't afraid of Dmitry or any of them. Thorn exited the building. "Ron!"

Ron was waiting by the vehicles after pulling them back behind the building. He knew it was only a matter of time before the two lieutenants decided to leave. The only way they were going to get that door open was if they acted as if they'd left.

"What is it?"

"Keep your eyes on Dmitry."

Ron looked past him towards where Dmitry was standing.

"Sure."

Although they had known each other for a while and Dmitry had helped him escape justice in America, he didn't trust him. He wasn't as worried about the missiles as he was about getting a bullet in the back of the head. The guy was volatile. He couldn't read him from one minute to the next. Dmitry had already killed others he'd worked alongside. He had serious trust issues, and worse than that, mental issues.

Thorn then tapped Ron. "When you're ready let's head in."

* * *

Sam had underestimated Richard's leverage in town. He'd managed to convince two police officers, and three local guys with military background to go with them. In the briefing, Blake had explained how he thought Thorn would try to launch the missiles, and how many they were up against. They piled into two trucks and tore out of there hoping to reach their destination just after nine that morning. Sam knew it would take longer than that due to the conditions of the road and having to pass through Denver but they'd stocked enough gasoline in canisters to get them there and back. They had mapped out two routes, one of which went east on I-70 and then north on I-25; the other would take them through Boulder.

For the most part they drove in silence.

Blake, a local guy by the name of Tim Snyder and a police officer rode with him while the others went in a separate vehicle.

"Why did you do it?" Sam asked.

Blake looked over. The steady rumble of the truck, and warm air pumping through the vents made them all look more tired than they were.

"I had no choice. He played me. Used my family."

"I can relate to that," Sam said.

"Your family still alive?" Blake asked.

"My daughter is. My ex-wife is dead."

"Sorry to hear that. Was it because of this?" he said looking out at the devastation.

"No. Heart issues."

"Oh."

There was silence for a while.

"Must be tough knowing that you were responsible for all of this," Sam said.

"Like I said, I had no choice."

"We always have a choice," Sam replied. "We just might not like the consequences."

"You'd let your daughter die so thousands could live?"

Sam shot him a glance. "What do you think I'm doing now?"

"I don't get it."

"My daughter is back in Breckenridge. I'm not. I can't protect her because I'm out here trying to stop whatever shit someone else started." He snorted. "It's like being in the military all over again. Placing the lives of others before my family."

"Is that why you signed up?"

"No, I just wasn't good at anything else," Sam replied.

"I can relate to that," Blake said.

The truck growled down the road. Sam thought about Anna and hoped she was okay. It seemed strange but after so many years of being outside of her life he worried more about her now than before. He pushed the gas pedal and the truck soared forward. His eyes scanned the horizon of orange, yellow and green, and the jagged mountains in the distance. They'd taken a few detours along the way due to blocked roads but hadn't encountered any hostiles, which was a relief after what he'd heard from Officer Somers.

"You know, I never imagined my career would lead me to this," Somers said.

"I don't think any of us did," Sam replied.

"What did you see last night?" Blake asked.

Somers stared out, lost in thought.

"Two of our officers were shot and killed. Guys I have worked alongside for years. People just turned and went crazy." Somers sighed. "And the hardest part about it is that I just stood there and watched, frozen by my own fear."

Both Sam and Blake shot him a glance.

"Like I wanted to do something but there were just too many. I drove away."

"What?" Sam asked, trying to wrap his head around that.

Somers looked at him, embarrassment made his cheeks go red. "I know I should have stayed but... in all my years in Breckenridge I've never had to deal with a riot situation. Sure, we've had protesters but they've always been peaceful, and the ones that weren't, well — you arrest a few and the rest disperse but not last night. It was like everyone lost their fucking minds. People thought we were lying to them."

Sam replied. "Everyone is conditioned to a certain way of living. They have expectations of how things should be, what they should have, their rights and so forth. There is a false sense of security. That's why they taught us to become comfortable in the uncomfortable because at any minute things can go tits up and you've got to be prepared to survive in the worst situations."

Somers nodded and ran a hand over his face. "I just thought our town would be different."

"Hey, look at it this way. It lasted a good ten days before it broke. It was going to happen one way or another. It was just a matter of time. Oneida, it was much faster."

"Tell me something," Somers asked. "You think there is hope for the country if we stop this?"

He gripped the steering wheel tight. They were driving through a canyon with high rock walls and large pine trees on either side. The landscape spread out before them as the sun rose in a deep blue sky. "Of course there is," Sam said. "If I didn't believe that, I wouldn't be here right now."

They continued on for several hours, each of them lost

in the regrets of days gone by. No one could change the past but what they did now would forever shape the future of not only their lives but the country as a whole.

Chapter 19

All he'd wanted was to strip away at the order Richard had established. Make him suffer for what he'd stolen from him — his livelihood, his reputation, and his home. Had the evening gone as planned, no harm would have come to him or his family but that was before his brother was hurt, and two of his friends killed.

Hours passed before they felt it was safe to enter.

After storming the house, and tearing it apart searching for Carl's shooter, he'd found the bloody handprint on the attic window, and several prints on the drainage pipe. Although he couldn't be sure they'd gone to the hospital, Carl needed medical attention so they opted to kill two birds with one stone and find out if anyone had arrived with a wound to the hand.

Leaving their weapons with Paul in the truck, Howard entered the hospital with Carl's arm draped over his shoulder. The four cops on the door had briefly questioned him but he said they'd been attacked in Breckenridge in a riot. And because they weren't packing heat, and Carl kept drifting in and out of consciousness, they let them in.

As soon as the doctors took over and wheeled him away, Howard and two of his men approached the front desk.

"Do you know what room they'll place him in?" Howard asked.

The nursed replied, "We should have an update for you shortly. If you want to take a seat over there I'll be sure to let you know."

"All right. Hey by the way, we had a neighbor of ours get shot in the hand. They're from Breckenridge. We were told they came here. Do you know what room they're in?"

"What's the full name?"

He turned to the other two and acted like he couldn't recall.

"I'm sorry. With my brother's injury I can't remember.

I believe the last name was Underwood."

She tapped a name into the computer and shook her head.

"Right. Um. Hold on a second," she said getting up and going over to one of her co-workers. It was a nurse. She turned and glanced at them and walked back.

"Sir, you don't know their full name?"

"I'm really sorry. It's on the tip of my tongue but… I only know the last name is either Underwood or Wade."

"Just give me a second."

She looked down at her computer and tapped a few keys. "We did receive in someone three hours ago. Anna Wade?"

He pulled a face and tapped the counter. "Anna. That's it. Damn, I would lose my head if it wasn't screwed on," he said.

The nurse chuckled. "Don't worry. Trust me, with everything that has happened over the past two weeks, I'm not exactly functioning at 100 percent either. Anyway, she's on the second floor, room 32. Would you like me to call up?"

"Ah no, we'll surprise her."

The ginger-haired lady nodded. "Did you say you were her neighbor?"

"Yeah, good friends with her grandfather."

"Okay, well, visiting hours are between eight and eight so if you want to go up, you can."

"I appreciate that, thanks," he said before turning to Liam and Jacob. "Jacob, tell Paul to bring the truck around to the emergency exit on the west side of the building. I think it's time we pay Anna a little visit."

"What about the cops?" Jacob asked.

Howard ran a hand around his neck. "Right, well let's handle them first."

* * *

Anna rolled her newly bandaged hand over. "They said I would need to stay so they can do surgery on the hand. They want to remove pieces of bone that are shattered. At least they gave me some serious pain medication."

"Happy juice?" Chase asked. "I could use some of that

right about now. It's crazy out in the halls. People are coming in with all manner of injuries. I overheard two people talking about a riot in Frisco. I'm telling you, Anna. Things are getting out of control. After we get out of here I think we should find your old man and see about leaving Breckenridge and heading to California."

"It's won't be any better there. It'll probably be worse," she said.

Chase ran a hand over his face and got up and went over to the window. He looked out and stared at the smoke spreading across the horizon. There was more than before. Even though the hospital was operating, he had to wonder how long it would last before tempers flared and people started lashing out at each other. He'd already seen two people having an argument with a nurse about not receiving treatment for close to seven hours. His mind drifted to his father and he wondered what he'd be doing now. If there were anyone who might have been able to weather an event like this, it would have been him. As he stared down into the parking lot, a stream of vehicles arrived, and people were being carried in with wounds to their faces.

"Holy crap. It's like a war zone out there," Chase said.

"I hope my father's okay."

"Yeah. I hope no one finds that rifle and handgun," he said.

"You buried them under those leaves. Relax," Anna said reaching over to get a glass of water. As Chase scanned the parking lot, he squinted as his eyes focused in on a truck that pulled up near the four police officers. One of the officers stepped up to the passenger side and said something and then pointed to what looked like bullet holes in the windshield.

It wasn't like it was an abnormal sight.

There were multiple vehicles in the parking lot that were peppered with holes.

But it wasn't that which caught his attention, it was the winch on the front. He thought back to the house and tried to remember what the color of the truck was. It was so dark last night but he was sure it had a sandy camouflaged appearance; similar to the one he was seeing now.

"Anna."

"Yeah?"

He stepped back for a second and observed the interaction with the cop. The truck driver slowly drove off and the officer returned to the group of cops who were milling near two cruisers. He breathed a sigh of relief thinking that he was becoming paranoid. It wasn't them. No. It couldn't be.

"Ah it's okay," he said. Chase was about to turn when the same truck reappeared tearing in from the west side and going at a high rate of speed directly at the cops.

The cops turned and two of them managed to leap out of the way, the other two weren't as fortunate. The truck hit them full speed, plowing them down. The other two officers went to open fire when three men walked into view behind them and opened fire. The cops' bodies flailed before dropping.

Chase's voice caught in his throat.

"Annnnna!"

He turned and grabbed her by her good hand and pulled her up out of bed. "Get up. Get up. We need to go. It's them…"

She tugged her arm away, and scowled. "What the hell are you on about?"

He pointed to the window and she crossed the room and looked out. Her jaw went slack. Suddenly, the faint staccato of gunfire could be heard down below followed by screams.

Anna was slipping into her sneakers while Chase kept an eye on the door. They were on the second level close to the east side of the building. Holding the door slightly ajar he glanced down the corridor and saw people exiting rooms, looking confused and distressed. There were two stairwells in the building and an elevator.

"Shit. I knew I should have brought that handgun," Chase said.

Both weapons were a good distance from the hospital. He'd buried them just inside the tree line in a spot he'd remember for when they got out. "Speed it up, Anna."

"I'm going as fast as I can."

"Forget the damn shoes."

She was struggling to get the second shoe on when he grabbed her hand and pulled her out of the room. They pushed forward through several patients who were heading the opposite way and were moving towards the east stairwell when a tall guy with a thick beard, armed with an AR-15, emerged from the stairwell. A family member of a patient lunged at him to try and wrestle the gun away. It was the worst thing he could have done. Two rounds and the brave individual slumped to the ground reeling in pain and gripping his stomach. The bearded guy stepped over him, only stopping for a second to put one more round in his head. Screams ensued, and the corridor filled up with people sprinting for the west side. Bullets whizzed overhead as people got in his way. Chase dragged Anna into the nearest room and closed the door. His heart was slamming against his chest, and his mind spinning out of control.

He hurried over to the window and looked out. They were too far up to jump. They would break their legs if they dropped and there was nowhere else to go.

"Shit. Shit. Think!" he said slapping his head a few times as if that would in some way clear the brain fog.

Anna was clutching her wrist and crouched down against the wall.

Chase sprinted over to the door and pulled it back ever so slightly. There were now two gunmen either side. A doctor tried to stop one of them and the other gunman unloaded a round from his shotgun blowing him back.

He closed the door. There was no lock to hold them back.

All they could do was wait and hope they didn't enter.

More gunfire erupted.

* * *

The only sound came from the generator, and the air pumping through the vents. Mia and Lieutenant Douglas stood on the metal grated bridge that separated the eight-ton blast door from the next. Strangely enough, Douglas had taken her outburst in stride. Whether it was because he'd encountered his fair share of feisty women or was too stressed out by their situation, he didn't dwell on her attacking him.

"What do you think?" she asked.

He shrugged. "Do we have any other choice?"

"You're asking me, after last night?"

"Mia, listen, I get it, you were trying to save your ass. I was just doing the same. I thought we had enough food and because they kept turning the air on and off I assumed they were playing head games."

She looked back at the second blast door.

"It's a gamble. We have a fifty-fifty chance they're on the other side." Mia exhaled hard. "They might be expecting us to come out of the escape hatch in which case they'd be topside but there still could be someone out there."

Mia walked back into the capsule and looked around. She unlocked the strap that held in their heavy aluminum coffee urn and took it out and handed it to Douglas.

"Here, take this."

"What are you doing?" he asked.

She didn't answer him but turned and went across the capsule to scoop up the arm-sized shovel. "Here's what we're going to do. I'll open the blast door and if they're on the other side, well, at least we tried."

Douglas stared down at the urn.

"You want me to make them coffee?"

She rolled her eyes not even wanting to answer that.

"Mia."

"Don't try to convince me not to open it. I'm doing it."

"I wasn't. I just wanted to apologize."

"For?"

"Everything."

"Shouldn't it be me apologizing?"

"In theory, yes. However, you probably wouldn't have lashed out had I listened to you or checked the damn food storage."

"You know, Douglas, you confuse the hell out of me."

With that said she went back out of the capsule and began the process of opening the final blast door. Her pulse sped up. She knew there was a very good chance of them being out there but that was a risk they had to take. Food they could last a long time without but water — nope.

"You ready?" she asked.

Douglas nodded, holding the heavy coffee urn.

The machinery clunked into place as the door unlocked and she pushed it open.

No sooner had she got it a few inches apart than the barrel of a gun pushed through the open gap. Mia froze but Douglas didn't. Out of sight, off to her right, he brought the urn down hard and fast on the tip of the gun. It erupted as a round fired, and the bullet ricocheted off the thick steel.

Mia charged forward without a thought to what lay beyond the door.

It all happened within a matter of seconds.

The barrel going down, the round firing and her

assault on the gunman.

"Douglas!" she yelled as she battered the man over the head with such speed and fury he didn't know what hit him. By the time he dropped, his face was covered in blood. Both of them landed on the man and looked around to see they were alone. It was just him down there.

Mia staggered to her feet, taking the rifle from the dead man.

Panting hard, she cleared the generator room and then looked at the elevator. While they were relieved to have made it out in one piece, it wasn't over yet. They still had the topside to deal with and if her gut instinct wasn't wrong, there were more of them up there. How many? That was to be seen.

One thing was for sure, she wasn't dying here. Not today. Not without taking as many of them with her as she could.

"If we can get up there, we can use the security phone to raise the alert," Douglas said peering up the elevator shaft then back at her.

She nodded. "I think I have a better idea."

* * *

Mason's eyes widened as he saw people streaming out of the hospital, some covered in blood. Several vehicles tore past him in a hurry. It was only when he got closer could he see the fallen officers. He slammed on the brakes and got out.

"Stay here," he said as he retrieved the M4 from the back of the trunk.

"I'm not staying," Amanda said. "I'm coming with you."

"Suit yourself but if you hesitate…"

"I know," she said.

Mason had shown her how to use a gun five days earlier. Out of their entire group Amanda had been the most gun shy but after all they'd experienced on the journey to Breckenridge she'd soon changed her tune. He'd taken her through some of the basics, helped her to understand that as long as she used it correctly and always treated it as though it was loaded, she'd be fine. Skill came through time, constant use and regular training and if the power grid remained down she'd have plenty of opportunity.

Chapter 20

Sam observed the unassuming missile alert facility through high-powered binoculars. It was out in the middle of nowhere — nothing but flat plains for miles. Besides the barbed wire fencing and several armored vehicles there really wasn't anything about the building that would have indicated that it was owned by the military. The main living quarters for security was a one-story clapboard structure with brown shingles. It had taken the better part of four hours to reach their destination.

"You sure this is it?" he asked.

"It's the closest one. There are only three active Minuteman III squadrons commanded by the 90th Operations Group. This one, Malmstrom in Montana and Minot in North Dakota."

"Not exactly well protected, is it?"

"The Launch Control Center is underground, it's

staffed by two officers, and a six-man security team. Additional backup is only a radio call away. I'd say that's well protected under normal circumstances."

"Yeah. Normal. And how many of these assholes did you say there were?"

"Roughly ten? At least that's what I can remember."

"You don't sound very sure," Sam said lowering the binoculars and looking at him.

"Sorry, I was slightly incapacitated after having endured days of torture. I was disoriented." He gritted his teeth.

Sam nodded. "And so… why did he leave you alive?"

"Said he wanted me to suffer."

"Why can't we all just get along," Sam muttered under his breath. He was standing in the bed of the truck leaning on the roof. He had a hand cupped over the top so the reflection of the glass didn't glint.

"You mind if I take a look?" Blake asked.

"Knock yourself out." Sam handed it to him and then went to the back of the truck and scooped up his M4 rifle. He looked at Somers who was standing nervously beside the truck. He'd seen the same look in the eyes of guys over in Iraq. It was one thing to want to be a soldier, it was another to face real danger. Being a small-town cop didn't exactly go hand in hand with combat experience. He'd considered joining a department out in California after he left the Navy but he really didn't fancy dealing with office politics, or knocking heads with those who were intimidated by his past résumé.

"You okay, Somers?"

He twisted around. "Yeah. So how we doing this?"

"Well I'd like to spend a day doing reconnaissance but there's no time for that shit." He smirked. "No, listen, the gates are wide open. It's not like we can take cover anywhere," he said looking at the open farmland. "So, we'll roll in while the other truck hangs back and provides additional cover from the east. I'm afraid there is no easy way to do this. We are up shit creek without a paddle. If we were in Iraq we'd have air support but I'm afraid it's just us and the metal on this vehicle is all we've got, so make good use of it."

Somers nodded as Sam hopped out of the truck and came around to the driver's side. Snyder was checking the ammo in his rifle.

"What's your background?" Sam asked.

"Infantry. I did nine years."

Sam watched him check over his rifle like he'd done it thousands of times. Under any other conditions he might have shot the breeze with him and swapped combat tales but all he wanted to do now was get in there and deal with the situation at hand. He went over to the second truck and updated them on the plan. Rich Michelson was the second police officer, and the two locals traveling with him went by their last names, Carlton and Jarvis.

"You sure you don't want us to follow you in?"

"Move in, just hanging back slightly. Once we're through those gates, stay to the east, and we'll approach via the south. We don't want to make this too easy for them."

He twirled a finger in the air.

"Gentlemen, let's move in."

* * *

The round tore through the armed assailant's skull dropping him instantly. Mason pressed in as the echo of gunfire dominated. They'd only made it a few feet inside the medical center when he'd encountered a hostile. Had he not shot him, he had no doubt in his mind he'd be the one laying on the ground.

Not everyone had run out of the building, some of the staff had taken cover behind the front desk. A security officer had been shot multiple times in the back as he'd tried to flee.

"How many more?" Mason asked a nurse cowering behind the desk.

She raised a hand. "Three. They went up."

Mason gestured to Amanda and they headed for the stairwell.

* * *

"They're not here!" the man bellowed. "I want them found." Chase closed the door. He'd watched one of them enter Anna's room only to come out a few seconds later. The other two men were going room to room, and at times dragging people out who tried to get in their way. The overflow of patients who had been lying on gurneys in the corridor were now cowering beneath them.

"We need to get the hell out of here," he said, approaching the window and sliding it open. A large gust of cold wind blew in and stole his breath. Chase leaned out and looked to his left and right, then up.

"I think we're going to have to jump."

"Are you crazy?" Anna replied.

"It's either that or we die. They're going room to room. It's only a matter—"

A flurry of rounds interrupted his train of thought. Chase dashed over to the door and pulled it back to see what was going on. A smiled flickered to life on his face at the sight of Mason. He'd killed one of the three men at the west side and had positioned himself by the doorway. Every few seconds he would bring the barrel of his rifle around and exchange lead. A female patient let out a high-pitched scream as one of the men grabbed her and backed up, using her as a human shield. The second guy was farther down pinned between them. He would unload then pull back into a room.

Chase watched as the second gunman dragged the woman back while opening fire on Mason. He was heading his way, trying to get to the east stairwell. Chase felt a surge of adrenaline and his mouth went dry. He knew what he had to do but his fear was out of control. Even with a weapon in hand he'd been paralyzed by his fear.

"Chase. What's going on?" Anna asked.

He waved her off, trying to summon the courage to do what was necessary, not just for the sake of Mason but also for the patient, and for both of them. He scanned the room looking for anything he could use as a weapon. There was a chair, and a stainless steel, heavy-duty IV pole.

Chase snatched up the pole and dashed back to the door.

Twenty feet.

Ten feet.

He pulled open the door, lifted the pole and waited.

His heart hammered in his chest.

Five feet.

"Chase," Anna called out.

He didn't respond, his focus was locked on the man. He knew the odds were stacked against him but he already had in mind what he was about to do. Another barrage of gunfire, and the woman screaming masked the sound of Chase's boots pounding the ground. The guy must have seen him at the last second, as he turned his head but it was too late. Chase jammed the sharpest end of the pole straight into the guy's face knocking him sideways into the open room across from them.

The rifle dropped out of his hands and clattered on the ground.

He didn't even think to ask Anna for help, he was too focused on surviving.

Blindsided, the guy didn't stand a chance. Chase

didn't give him a second to recover. He began pounding his face with the pole multiple times until he stopped moving. When he finally stepped back, the guy was barely alive.

Chase turned for the gun but it was no longer there.

Anna had scooped it up and was attempting to provide additional cover for Mason from the safety of the doorway. She fired two rounds then pulled back.

Chase motioned for her to toss it to him, instead she slid it across the floor.

In an instant, he pulled it around, fired a round into the guy on the floor to put him out of his misery and then tried to get a bead on the third gunman.

* * *

Howard barricaded himself in the private medical room using what little furniture he could find, his mind running rampant. It wasn't meant to end this way. He slung his rifle behind his back and crossed over to the window and slid it open. As he was facing the north side, there was a portion of the roof that jutted out but it was a good twenty-foot drop. He turned and ran through his options. He could try and fight his way out or take his chances and jump. He weighed the odds. Two of them were armed, and there was only him now.

Four rounds speared his door making the decision for him.

Howard secured the rifle around his back, climbed up onto the ledge and tried to lower himself. He wasn't a tall man, just a little over five foot four, so it wasn't like it would make much difference but it was better than just launching himself out.

The cold fall wind whipped at his clothes and in those final seconds he regretted ever stepping foot inside Breckenridge. More rounds erupted followed by the sound of them trying to force their way inside. Howard released his grip and dropped.

* * *

After Mason shouldered his way into the room, he fully expected one last attack but it wasn't to be. "Where is he?" Chase asked, then they saw the drapes in front of the window swaying in the breeze.

They darted over and Mason looked out

He winced, not seeing any movement.

It was a grim sight.

"Is he dead?" Chase asked.

"If he isn't, he's at the right place to get treatment."

Chapter 21

Mia wasn't a fool. She knew the second they went up in that elevator the rest of the terrorists would execute them, so they sent the elevator up with the dead man in it. Below ground they listened for the sound of gunfire, an immediate reaction to seeing their fallen comrade.

Nothing.

Not a bullet fired.

Not even a footstep.

"It's possible they left him here while they took off."

"What, to go and get coffee?" Mia said, shaking her head. "C'mon, Douglas. They're up there."

He shook his head. "I don't hear a damn thing. If they are outside or have left to get something I don't want to lose the window of opportunity." Douglas scooped up the dead man's rifle. "I'm going up," he said hitting the button to bring the elevator back down.

Mia placed a hand on his shoulder. "Hold on a

second, Douglas."

"Mia. You were the one biting at the bit to get out of here. It was your idea to exit."

"Yeah so we can live. We need to play this smart. They'll be expecting us to head up. So we exit via the escape tunnel."

"That was your great idea? Geesh!" Douglas shook his head in disbelief.

She fired back. "Well it's not like we have many options. It's the elevator, stay in the capsule with zero supplies or the escape tunnel."

Douglas tilted towards her. "I already told you. The chances of you getting through that hard soil are slim to none and if they get their hands on you, it's game over." He looked back at the elevator as it reached the ground and let out a clunk. He tapped the gun. Douglas pulled open the steel gates ready to go up.

"Just stay down here. If you hear any shooting, lock yourself in the capsule."

"Douglas."

"I'll be fine. The security control center is within spitting distance when I reach the top. I'll make contact with backup and be down in minutes."

He stepped into the elevator and pulled the gates shut. Through the slats of metal she watched him adjust his grip on the rifle, and do a quick ammo check. He gave a short nod, and then hit the button.

Mia watched until the elevator disappeared out of view.

The elevator made a whirring sound that echoed through the depths of the shaft until it jerked to a stop. She heard the gates pull back and Douglas step out but no gunfire. Was it possible they'd left? Or were they just playing mind games?

A sudden eruption of gunfire answered that.

Not wasting a second, she darted into the capsule and sealed it closed.

"Shit. Shit! Why didn't you listen to me?" she muttered. Sure the soil was hard but it was coming away when she had begun picking at it. Besides, there was no sign pointing where the opening was on the surface. Mia hurried over to the ladder and scurried back into the tube and began hacking away at the soil with the shovel.

She hadn't managed to scrape more than a few chunks when the phone began ringing. Mia ignored it and continued scraping until it started ringing again.

Staring down into the capsule she climbed down and reluctantly picked up the phone.

"Lieutenant Hart, or would you prefer I call you Mia?"

"And you are?"

"Thorn."

"What do you want?"

"C'mon. And I thought you were the smart one."

"Is he dead?"

Thorn snorted. "Who, Douglas?" He chuckled. "No. Well, not yet. But he sure is lonely up here. How about you take that pretty ass of yours and come and join him."

She heard Douglas yell, "Don't do it, Mia!"

His voice was quickly muffled. It sounded like they had struck him.

"Do the right thing, lieutenant. Enough games. You now decide if Douglas lives or dies."

With that said he hung up.

* * *

Outside the echo of gunfire carried on the wind. Sam's truck was closing in on the property when he'd heard it. He'd swerved the vehicle at an angle not far from the building. All of them exited and had taken cover behind it assuming they were the target. As the minutes rolled on, it didn't take long to realize they weren't.

"What do you think?" Tim asked. He was lying prone near the driver's side with a rifle aimed at the main door. Somers had taken a knee at the rear and kept poking his head out.

Sam didn't reply, instead he turned and motioned for the second vehicle to make its way up. A large plume of dust billowed up behind it as it rumbled up the final stretch of road. No sooner had he turned back to respond to Tim than several men streamed out of the building with their weapons at the ready.

One glance their way, and all hell broke loose.

Bullets whistled overhead, and speared the truck like a heavy downpour of hailstones. They didn't hesitate to return fire. Tim was the first to react, taking one of them down after squeezing off a burst.

Sam felt his heart catch in his chest as he engaged. He turned his head briefly to see Officer Michelson swerve the second vehicle over to where there was a Humvee, and several other vehicles. All three men jumped out — Carlton and Jarvis fanned out using the corner at the far end of the building as cover, while Michelson opted for the back of his truck. He hopped into the bed and pulled up to the cab, resting his police-issued AR-15 on top. They were all taking a huge risk, but the consequences of failure would be devastating.

Gravel crunched below their feet as Sam shifted position and waited for the next wave. He could hear men yelling orders, then several windows were shattered, and the tips of barrels jutted out.

"Get down!" Sam yelled just as rounds lanced the side

of the truck, peppering it from back to front. The front tire hissed, and the frame rattled as they drilled it with everything they had.

Somers yanked a smoke grenade off his flak jacket, twisted and tossed it between them and the building. A heavy white smoke burst out flooding the grounds like a ghostly apparition.

"I'm..." Snyder was about to say something as he rolled to one side to reach for another magazine only to be struck in the head by a round. His body went limp and Blake Dawson dropped down and took his spot. There was no time to mourn.

More rounds pinged off metal and tore up the gravel all around them.

Blake sprawled out and shifted Tim's body up as additional cover.

* * *

"Who the fuck are these guys?" Dmitry yelled unleashing a flurry of rounds from the doorway. He pulled back, tossed a magazine and palmed another in.

Thorn inched up to a window and zoomed in on the truck. For a second he couldn't see anything beyond the odd head that would emerge then disappear, or a barrel firing. Then his eyes fell upon the familiar face of Blake Dawson. A shot of panic went through him at his mistake, and the thought of the situation now spiraling out of control. He should have killed him but he wanted him to suffer. *Shit!* Up until that point, they'd hit a road bump but they were making progress, in fact they were moments away from gaining entry to the capsule.

"No matter what. They are not to get in here," he bellowed turning back to the phone and calling down again. He grasped hold of the battered and bruised lieutenant and dragged him over to the phone. He put a Glock against the side of his head and waited for her to answer.

"Hello?"

"Twenty seconds. If I don't hear that elevator in the next twenty seconds, I will personally put a bullet through his skull. You hear me!" he yelled then glanced out the window to stay abreast of the situation.

"Is he even alive?" Mia asked.

Thorn jabbed the phone at Douglas. "Mia, don't…"

He wouldn't let him tell her what was occurring topside otherwise she might have been less inclined to leave the capsule. "Fourteen seconds. Choose wisely, lieutenant."

He slammed the phone down and dragged Douglas over to the elevator shaft.

"You won't succeed," Douglas mumbled, blood trickling out the corner of his mouth and down his jaw. He was on his knees, barely able to summon the strength to fight back because they'd beaten him so badly.

Thorn ignored him. "Nine seconds. Looks like your co-worker doesn't think too highly of you."

"Fuck you."

Thorn continued counting down in his head. As he got to about five, Douglas lunged at him nearly causing him to fall into the shaft. A few seconds of struggling, a feeble attempt to be a hero before Thorn battered him across the top of his head.

Before he'd reached the end of the countdown he fired a round into his skull.

Almost immediately he heard the churn of the elevator.

Thorn scrambled back and kicked Douglas's body into the shaft.

There was a large thud as the rising elevator broke his fall.

With his gun aimed at the shaft he expected to see her, instead it was empty.

"Bitch!" he yelled.

* * *

Like the earth giving birth to new life, Mia burst out of the grassy grave near a satellite dish, her face covered in dirt. Douglas was wrong. All the time she'd been down there she'd worked away at the three feet of soil until she saw a shard of daylight break through, and the rest collapsed inward allowing her to escape.

The capsule was still sealed making sure that asshole

couldn't use it.

Her heart skipped a beat at the sound of gunfire. At first she thought they were shooting at her but as she crawled out, clawing her way to freedom, she turned to find six men attacking the facility.

A volley of rounds chewed up the structure, and the landscape.

At first she had no idea who they were until she spotted two police uniforms.

Unsure but open and exposed to the bullets whizzing through the air, Mia sprinted towards the truck at a crouch. Her fears were soon relieved as the cop waved her towards them. She raced behind the truck and gripped hold of the cop as if the nightmare was over.

It was far from over.

Rounds cut into the truck, the echo of an M4 was deafening.

* * *

"Ma'am, is there anyone else in there?" Sam asked.

Her chin dropped and she shook her head.

"He's trying to get into the bunker," Dawson said firing off a few more rounds.

"He won't be able to. It's sealed. The only way in is through the escape hatch now," Mia replied.

"He can still launch it," Dawson said.

"He won't," she said confidently. Dawson shot her a glance. "If he wanted to, he would have done it by now. Without immediate protection it would be suicide."

Sam had no qualms about him being crazy enough to do it but not all terrorists were willing to die for a cause. Was he?

"Get her out of here," Sam said to Dawson realizing they were in the crosshair and receiving the bulk of the assault. "We'll cover you," he said ripping off a smoke grenade from his jacket. He twisted, pulled and launched it over the top of the truck into the kill zone. Two tires were down, all the windows shattered on the truck and the panels must have looked like a colander.

All three of them focused on the door and windows as a steady onslaught of rounds echoed loudly.

* * *

After confirming the capsule was sealed, Thorn returned to the surface and staggered back into the hallway to find only four of his men still alive. Gunfire continued, rounds tearing up the lot beyond the doors. Dmitry pulled away from the entrance. "Thorn! Give the order to launch now!"

He shook his head, no.

It was one thing to bring the grid down and send the nation into chaos, another to know when it no longer served a purpose. While his hatred for the U.S. ran deep, as did Dmitry's for Russia, he knew, as he did when the NSA first caught him, when it was time to bounce.

If launching the missiles meant he could escape he would have done so in a heartbeat but this was now out of his control, and he wasn't ready to die — just as he wasn't prepared to go to prison. Not now. Not for the USA and not for Russia.

"No, we leave now," he said.

Dmitry scowled. "Leave?" He towered over him. "I did

not come this far, or lose this many men to turn back now." He charged past Thorn and scooped up the radio and began barking orders.

"Come in, Niles…"

Before he could spit the rest out, Thorn plowed into him, making him drop the radio. He cracked him with several blows to the jaw and delivered a hard uppercut but it barely fazed him. Dmitry spat blood on the floor, and went for his handgun.

Thorn was already one step ahead of him.

He finished him with two shots to the heart.

Dmitry slumped to the floor and then Thorn got on the radio.

"Niles. Meet me at the highway."

"But."

"The mission is compromised," he bellowed. "It's time to leave."

Thorn didn't inform the others, they were the distraction. None of them were brothers, close friends or anyone he gave two shits about. They were joined only by

342

their hatred for the government and their expertise in hacking.

He grabbed his rifle and headed out the rear.

Attempting to reach the trucks, which had been brought around the side, wouldn't work; all he could hope for was that the other guys would hold them at bay long enough for his escape to remain unknown.

* * *

Dawson ran at a crouch, eyes flitting towards the structure as they made it to the second truck. Michelson tossed him the keys and joined the other two while he reversed out, heading backward towards the gate. The truck let out a loud whining sound as he leaned back and smashed his foot on the accelerator.

Just as he swerved it out of the gate, kicking up a curtain of dust, he jerked the wheel to his left and his eye caught a lone figure darting across the flatlands that framed the facility. Dawson squinted. Although the person had put some distance between himself and the building, he was certain he knew who it was — Thorn.

That coward.

A swell of pain from losing his son and wife gripped him and he jammed the gearstick in drive and took off in pursuit going around the facility and bumping out onto the open plain. In the distance, Thorn cast a glance over his shoulder and broke into an all-out sprint but it was pointless. Dawson blocked out the sound of Mia, the gunfire behind him and all reasoning — only the drive to kill him dominated.

Within seconds the truck closed the gap. It roared as it raced across the field, and Dawson bounced in his seat. As they got closer, Thorn turned, squeezed off rounds, a desperate attempt to survive the inevitable.

It failed.

Dawson relished the thud, and crunch of the truck as it plowed over him.

He glanced over his shoulder, stuck the gear into park and hopped out.

Thorn squirmed across the ground, moaning and dragging his limp body. Dawson thought of Kelly, and

Aidan's final moments — the look of pure terror in their eyes, and the knowledge that they were about to die. He wanted Thorn to taste that.

This was for them.

Upon reaching him, Dawson looked down, shaking his head, unable to believe that this one person could be responsible for the downfall of a nation. Thorn rolled over, dirt clinging to his clothes. He stared up with pitiful eyes, his lips opening as if to beg for mercy.

He wouldn't give it.

Without another word, Dawson crouched and removed the knife from the sheaf wrapped around Thorn's leg. He rolled it in his hand a couple of times letting the glint of the sun catch his eye before he said, "You should have killed me."

Dawson heard air catch in Thorn's throat as he lunged forward, slashing his throat. Blood gushed out, and he made a choking sound. He wanted him to know what his son suffered. He wanted to see the same hopelessness in his eyes that Aidan had.

He saw it.

There in the middle of nowhere, he listened as Thorn took his last breath.

Dawson scooped up Thorn's rifle nearby and returned to the vehicle, satisfied but broken.

Chapter 22

Five Days Later

In the aftermath of the raid on the missile launch facility, only two of Thorn's ten men survived, and they surrendered without incident. Niles Black and Garrett Forester were found waiting beside the highway for Thorn to return — the look of surprise when Sam's team showed up was priceless. What Sam came to understand from Dawson was that this wasn't a group of suicidal terrorists, hardened criminals that had any form of combat training — they were opportunists, hackers, guys that usually operated alone. In fact that was why his team had been successful in taking back the facility with minimal loss of life. It was the reason why neither Niles nor Garrett put up a fight when they came upon them.

Dawson didn't say much about how Thorn died

except to say that he no longer posed a threat. They returned Lieutenant Hart to the facility and established radio contact with the military.

Within the hour, several Black Hawks arrived from Cheyenne Mountain Air Force Station to relieve her of her position, to secure the perimeter, and to take Blake Dawson back with the hope of using his expertise to bring the grid back up.

It was the last time Sam would ever see Blake.

Their farewell was as brief as their meeting. Blake shook hands with those he'd fought alongside and promised he would do everything within his means to turn back the tide.

Upon return to Breckenridge, they weren't greeted like heroes. Few knew of the operation. For Sam this was normal but he could tell some of the group had expected the streets to be full of cheering people. The reality was they received nothing more than a pat on the back by Chief Sanchez. There was no reward to be had as in reality their circumstances hadn't changed.

Tim Snyder was handed back to his family for burial. They opted to keep the funeral private, so few words were exchanged that day but Sam told them he didn't die in vain and his name would always be remembered.

Sam was horrified to learn about Anna's injury but overcome with gratitude for the brave actions of Chase, Amanda and Mason. They'd all come a long way, overcome dangerous obstacles and were stronger for it.

"Are you sure you won't come with us?" Chase asked Sam.

Over the past twenty-four hours Chase had brought up the conversation again about journeying to California. He was eager to see if his family was safe. Although it had been Sam's initial goal to return to California, his situation with Anna had changed.

With the town still without power, Sam had accepted a temporary position with Breckenridge Police Department. Although the city didn't have much to offer, the resolve of the officers at that department had proven that good still existed in light of all that had transpired. It gave him hope for the future even if it was in darkness.

Despite the riots and fires that occurred days earlier, town residents showed a surprising show of force for good. Like a man pushed into a corner, the town revealed its true colors under duress and fought back. Fires were extinguished. Trouble makers were arrested, and home invasions dwindled. Breckenridge as a community was stronger than he thought. It was stronger than the few that attempted to take advantage of it at its weakest time. It was for these reasons and more that he decided to stay.

Sam stood beside Anna with his arm around her shoulder. "Thanks but no. My home is here. It always has been. And if there was ever a time this place could use some help, it's now."

Although a section of Helen's home had been destroyed by fire, it wasn't anything that he didn't think he could fix. The local lumber company and hardware stores in town had stepped up to the plate and offered those whose homes had been damaged, the tools, supplies and equipment needed to rebuild.

Those who'd lost homes were offered temporary housing in real estate that was empty. Although Sam knew that not every town or city would come together and work for the good of each other, it encouraged him to see it in Breckenridge.

Chase shook Sam's hand, and got into the derby car.

"You sure we can't convince you to come?" Mason asked Amanda.

She shook her head. "No, but if you ever make it back this way again, be sure to drop in, okay?"

He smiled and gave her a warm hug before Amanda headed back into the house with Anna. Mason stood in front of Sam, a smirk appearing on his face.

"Well sir, it has been one hell of a ride."

"That it has," Sam replied.

He extended a hand and Sam pulled him in and gave him a hug. "Stay safe out there, my friend. You hear me?"

"Always."

They pulled away from each other.

"I hope he doesn't annoy you too much," Sam said

with a head nod to Chase.

"If he does…" Mason tapped the Glock in his holster and they both laughed. "You going to be okay here?"

Sam looked back at the house. "I think so."

"No, I meant with dickhead." He smiled.

"Richard? Oh, you didn't hear?"

Mason's brow pinched. "Hear what?"

Sam got this devilish grin on his face. "Keith Boone — you know, Howard's brother — tried to strike up a plea deal to get a lesser sentence for his involvement in the attempted shooting at the town hall meeting. Which I might add was later confirmed by several witnesses. He told Chief Sanchez a number of toe-curling stories about Richard's involvement with him and his brother. It seems Richard's influence and power in this community has come to an end."

"They've arrested him?"

"Not exactly. It depends on what evidence they find in Howard's home. But rumor has it Keith said he could lead them to a vault of damning evidence. Seems it's not the first time their paths have crossed. So who knows what he's responsible for? All I know is that no one has seen Richard in over three days. Let's hope it stays that way."

"Huh! Coward probably fled," Mason said.

Sam nodded. "Let's hope so."

Mason breathed in deeply, patted him on the shoulder then gave a salute and headed for the car.

"Hey, Mason."

He turned. "Yeah?"

"You think you'll ever return?"

The corner of his lip curled up. "I don't know... Colorado can sure be cold in the winters. And I hear the California sun can be quite addictive."

Sam laughed.

Mason jabbed his finger. "But if the lights come back on. You have my word."

He winked and slipped into the driver's side. Sam listened as the two of them began to bicker like two old ladies. Mason fired up the engine.

"Hey you think I can drive?" Chase said.

"You at the wheel? Over my dead body," Mason said.

Sam chuckled as Mason honked the horn and pulled out. He stood a moment longer looking out into the darkness, the smell of pine lingering in the air. A cold breeze blew in chilling him to the bone. The nation had been without power for over two weeks, he'd witnessed towns crumble and communities fight back. They'd seen the desperation of many and the brave determination of the few. There was no telling when or if the power would ever come back on again. The fate of the country now relied on the goodwill of other nations, and the expertise of Blake Dawson, a man who had for a second time shown that where there was a will, there was a way.

"Hey dad," Anna called out. "You ready to eat?"

Sam looked over his shoulder, nodded and turned to head in.

As he began strolling towards the door, the lights in the house blinked on.

Anna twisted and frowned. "What the heck?"

"Did you fire up the generator?" Sam asked.

She responded no with a shake of the head.

Sam glanced off to his right, through the trees he noticed the faint glow of yellow coming from a neighbor's house. He put up a finger and walked briskly to the end of the driveway. As he rounded a cluster of trees and came out onto the main road, his eyes widened at the sight of more homes. All the lights were on. *Can it be? Oh God, please.* His pulse sped up as he broke into a jog and climbed up a section of hillside to get a better view of the town at the base of the Rocky Mountains. Sam clambered over a rise and smiled thinking of Dawson's promise.

At the top his question was answered.

"You did it," he said.

Sam breathed heavily, as he caught his breath and soaked it all in.

A multitude of lights across the landscape flickered on like a thousand fireflies.

* * *

THANK YOU FOR READING

As We Break: (Book 2)

This was the final book in the duology.

Please take a second to leave a review, it's really

appreciated. Thanks kindly, Jack.

A Plea

Thank you for reading As We Break. If you enjoyed the book, I would really appreciate it if you would consider leaving a review. Without reviews, an author's books are virtually invisible on the retail sites. It also lets me know what you liked. You can leave a review by visiting the book's page. I would greatly appreciate it. It only takes a couple of seconds.

Thank you — **Jack Hunt**

Newsletter

Thank you for buying As We Break, published by Direct Response Publishing.

Click here to receive special offers, bonus content, and news about new Jack Hunt's books. Sign up for the newsletter. http://www.jackhuntbooks.com/signup/

About the Author

Jack Hunt is the author of horror, sci-fi and post-apocalyptic novels. He currently has three books out in the War Buds Series, Four books out in the EMP Survival series, Two books in the Against all Odds duology, Two books in the Wild Ones series, three in the Camp Zero series, five books out in the Renegades series, three books in the Agora Virus series, and several single novels. There is one called Blackout, one called Final Impact, one called Darkest Hour, one out in the Armada series, a time travel book called Killing Time and another called Mavericks: Hunters Moon. Jack lives on the East coast of North America.

CPSIA information can be obtained
at www.ICGtesting.com
Printed in the USA
FSHW011956081118
53672FS

9 781726 039703